LOVE'S BETRAYAL 2

A Corrupt Love Affair

TAJA MORGAN WITHDRAWN

Love's Betrayal 2
Copyright 2019 by Taja Morgan

Published by Mz. Lady P Presents

PROLOGUE | HIS BLOOD IS ON YOUR HANDS

In a semi-darkened haze, the smell of death lingered through my nostrils as I struggled with seeing where I was. A pain erupting from within my womb caused me to clutch my oversized belly as blood coated both of my hands. With no knowledge of where this unknown blood had come from, I rubbed my eyes trying to see my way through the darkness.

"Is anybody there?" My voice echoed as the overwhelming, eerie silence caused chills to cascade down my spine. Partially frightened, I started to walk as far as my legs would allow until this chilling, evil laugh had come from out of nowhere.

"Who the fuck is there? This shit is not funny!"

"Tsk, tsk, tsk," the familiar tone of voice spoke. Emerging from the darkness, Hasaan stood before me with a sadistic smile. "I think it's about time you got a dose of your own personal hell, my love."

Warping into another dimension, much darker, the laughs had grown louder as blood from my wound began to pool underneath me. With the pain ripping through like a bullet ricocheting throughout my body, my mind went entirely to this child growing inside of me. Tears burned my eyes, followed by what felt like real fire forming inside my womb as I fell to my knees.

"His blood is on your hands." Gen B appeared, laughing and pointing. "His blood is on your hands."

"My baby, you're hurting my baby!" I screamed.

"His blood is on your hands," Hasaan joined.

Standing beside each other, they eagerly looked upon me as I let out a guttural scream, wanting it all to come to an end.

"His blood is on your hands," they continued.

"Baby?"

"Yaz?" Appearing and looking so angelic, he was dressed in all white as he bent down to grab my face. "Baby, you have to help me."

"Why'd you do it, Lem?"

"Yaz, help me! I don't know what the fuck you're talking about!"

Once those words escaped my lips, his persona had changed, and his angelic demeanor had immediately switched to a bloody, evil type of red as anger filled his eyes. In his hands, he held a gun and pointed it at me as Jhea and Indie stood at both sides of him.

"His blood is on your hands," they chanted, joining Hasaan and Gen B.

"Yasir, no baby please, I'm begging you!"

"My blood is on your hands," he stated calmly, squeezing the trigger.

Screaming and fighting against the pain, this overwhelming feeling of someone holding onto me caused me to lash out even more as I continued to cry out.

"Baby, look at me!"

Opening my eyes one by one, Yaz held my face full of concern as I looked around, realizing we were in our bedroom, and it was only a dream. Overwhelmed and terrified at the point that everything had felt entirely too real, I sobbed into his chest as he rubbed my back and held me.

"I'm sorry, baby. I'm so sorry."

"Shhh, calm down. It wasn't real. It was just a dream. You're okay, a'ight. I got you. Always and forever, remember?"

"No," I cried, shaking my head. "There was a gun and our baby... they tried to hurt our fuckin' baby!"

"Nobody's hurting you or the baby, maw. It was just a dream," he stated, rubbing my stomach. "It was just a dream, Halima. Calm down."

"Yasir, you don't understand. They—"

"Nobody's hurting you or our baby, Lem. Your hormones all over the place, you're stressed out and pregnant as fuck," he stressed, cracking a smile as he held my face. "It's a lot to handle, I know, but I got you. It's okay. I'm right here at your side, and I won't ever allow no nigga or bitch to hurt you. Okay?"

"You promise?"

"I promise my love. Now let's go back to sleep, you need your rest. Okay?"

"Okay."

Chapter One

HALIMA "LEMY" HODGE

"Yasir!" I screamed as the smoke detectors ranging throughout our home.

Hurriedly rushing and throwing my robe over my nude body, I securely held my stomach and dashed out the room. Arriving downstairs, Yaz stood over the stove fanning away the smoke as I calmed down.

"I could've sworn I told your no cooking ass to stay the fuck away from the stove," I fussed.

"You got jokes?"

"Where'd you put the broom?"

"Daddy's sorry," he spoke sincerely, bending down to kiss my stomach. "I ain't mean to disturb y'all. I just wanted to surprise you."

"I'd be better off if you left the stove alone, please and thank you," I teased, pressing my lips to his. "What time is Gen B coming over?"

"She should be pulling up at any minute, but I'ma let you know now. Don't be on that bullshit with your moods, not today, Lem."

"I'll just stay upstairs, problem solved."

With my due date slowly nearing, the time was out for the bullshit, and I simply had no patience for utter ignorance. Sadly, my mother-in-law and I will never see eye to eye, which I am completely okay with. I refuse to bend over backwards trying in more ways than one to make myself likable by a woman who is set in her ways.

Yaz was a peacemaker. He literally hated anything close to drama, and it practically shows. To avoid having him in the middle of turmoil, I've kept my distance. My mood depends on how I feel. Plus, today was one of my irritating days, and a bitch currently wasn't in the mood for any judgment.

As if on cue, the doorbell began to ring as I rolled my eyes. Sensing my frustration while fixing my food, which was some leftovers I'd cooked on yesterday, he kissed my jaw and went to get the door. Tying my robe being that I was naked underneath, Gen B's voice filled our home as I prepared myself for whatever.

"Halima."

"Hey, Gen B."

"Getting close to that time, isn't it?"

"Yep, just about."

"You two picked out a date yet?" she questioned. "I know Yasir was saying how you two were playing around with some for quite some time now."

"January first of next year, right baby?"

"Yea, it marks new beginnings and I wouldn't wanna bring the new year in any other way," he spoke wholeheartedly.

"You two don't have much time. That is cutting it kind of close."

"Well, it's what we agreed together, and that's what the date will be."

"This is all new to you, Halima," she stated, stepping closer. "Not only will this be a change for us, but it'll also be a change for you as well. I want the absolute best for my son, I—"

"Mama."

"With all due respect Gen B, I'm well aware of everything happening to me. I don't need you dictating what I do and who I do it with because I'm a grown woman. I don't have a mother nor do I have a father, and I think I'm doing very well for myself without either, so I really appreciate the concern, but I don't need it."

"Baby, this world is gonna chew you up and spit your ass out."

"And you honestly think I give a fuck what you gotta say about me or how you feel?"

"Halima!"

"How do we know this isn't all a get rich scheme to trap my son? You think I don't know how you guttural gold diggers are?" she questioned. "I know your type, and I know it all too well. You two broke up, and when you come back, you're pregnant? Oh girl, that child you're carrying will have a blood test done whenever it gets here."

"Bitch, don't you ever speak on my child!"

"Ah, there are her true colors."

"Fuck you and Yaz. Get your fuckin' hands off me because this is the shit I be talking about, and you wonder why I feel the way I do. Fuck you and her!"

Storming off to our bedroom with my food in tow, I slammed the door. My blood was boiling, and I was angry that I couldn't knock that bitch out. Hearing the truth of the severity of this situation just put it all into perspective, because deep down, I wanted so badly for this child to be Yaz's, but I also knew there was a slim chance it could also be Hasaan's child.

Although things seemed pristine and cookie cutter between us, I hated how his mother literally dictated everything about our relationship. I understand Yaz and Gen B have this untouchable bond, but I was now Yaz's woman. I was damn sure going to fight for my relationship, even if it took every breath in me. In my eyes, there was no breaking up, and the moment this nigga got down on his knee, all thoughts of ending things were now no longer.

"Don't bring your ass in here telling me what I did wrong because I didn't do shit," I fussed. Yaz entered the room looking like he had it on his mind to start an argument.

"I asked you, man. I asked you to keep it cool."

"And she tried me! What the fuck was I supposed to do? See, you got me fucked up because you're used to a bitch doing as you say, but that ain't me. As a matter of fact, get the fuck outta my face because your real-life disgusting me."

"You're dismissing me after that shit you pulled down there? Why you can't just do as I fuckin' say, Halima?"

"Because I'm your woman, not some fuckin' random ass hoe, and I wish you'd stop treating me as such! You wanna know why I stay in my place. It's because you can't take up for me, and it's every single time with her Yasir, I'm fuckin' tired of coming second to your mother! I am carrying your child for crying out loud, or do you feel the same way she does?"

"When have you ever heard me say that, huh? I do all that I can. I work hard as fuck to make a life for you! I know how she is, but you gotta see past that shit. Baby, I'm so fuckin' sorry she treats you the way that she does," he stated calmly. "I love you. When have I ever doubted or not believed you?"

"Stop beating around the bush when we've been avoiding this for months." I shrugged, moving out of his grasp. "Do you want this test done or what, Yasir?"

"If I wanted the test done, I would've told you to get it done, Lem."

"Don't lie to me."

Letting my guard down with my real emotions on full display, which is something I rarely ever did, I was stripped away and faced with a man who had accepted my all. As much as I wanted our lives to be as perfect as everything was before he'd met me, unfortunately, that wasn't the case for me.

"We can't be stress-free in the present if we're still dwelling on this past, Lem."

ॐ

That night, he didn't come to bed at his regular time, and I was unable to rest comfortably. My curiosity had gotten the best of me as I ventured out of bed. My heightened sense of smell immediately caught a whiff of weed as I found him closed off in his office, smoking a blunt as I pushed the door open. Seated shirtless with his tattoos on full display, his low eyes met mine as I sighed.

"You don't need to be all around this shit. Close the door, and I'll be in the room in a minute."

"You only smoke when you're stressed. What's going on?"

"Why you gotta be so hardheaded?"

"Because I love you and I care, plus I'm not about to let my man use weed to confront whatever the fuck is bothering him," I admitted. "Talk to me. Just like if something were bothering me, you'd pull it out of me."

"Just some work-related shit," he spoke as I placed myself onto his lap. "Nothing too outta the ordinary and nothing for my beautiful woman to be worried about."

Truth be told, I often worried about Yaz. His routine was simple, and he didn't really switch up until I'd entered his life, which meant some change had to take place. The changes I've seen within him, I am very thankful, but I couldn't help but think of the downsides.

With everything we've been through, I saw a side of him like never before and as odd as it may seem, it frightened me. I was afraid of the reality of what lingered behind the true Yasir Cosart because he never really stepped away from that perfect rep of his. I was only given a glimpse of it, but it was just enough for me to know that I couldn't fuck this up.

Chapter Two

YASIR "YAZ" COSART

"Would you like a refill, sir?"

"Oh nah, I'll take water."

"She got you on an alcohol cleanse too?" Indie laughed, shaking his head. "Damn, so this is what the fuck it means to be in love, huh?"

In between preparing for the baby and adjusting to becoming this whole new man in only a matter of months had come with the ultimate distance being placed in between Indie and me. We were brothers, and no matter how much time has passed, we'd always be thick as thieves. It's been that way for years.

Unfortunately, Indie didn't grow up with a family, so my folks had taken him under their wing. I've seen him at his lowest, his highest, and I wanted nothing but the best for my brother. Though we were of no blood relation, our bond had run deeper than anything. Judging by his distance, I could tell he didn't quite agree with my moving so fast with Lem, but we lived two different lives, and that was just the reality of it.

"Here you go. I don't even need to get you fuckin' started, dawg."

"Y'all figure out what it is yet?"

"The gender reveal/ baby shower is gonna be sometime in April. She's due in May, so we gotta get a move on."

"Is moms good with all this too?"

"Hell nah, man. They're always arguing and shit." I sighed. "I get tired of the shit honestly, but I just feel like mama's gotta fall back. We both know how she is."

"Yea, she's a force, dawg. You deserve it though, man. After all, I have never seen shit ever get so serious like this. You ain't even proposed to Bri."

"Lem is different. I can't describe it, but she gets me. Brielle and me, it wasn't meant to be. There's a lot of shit you'on know about that relationship, but shit was toxic as fuck."

For years, I've avoided the topic of discussing my troubles I'd undergone throughout my relationship with Brielle. Ultimately, I was always taught that certain people brought out the bad in you, but it never did make any sense until I'd crossed paths with her. We'd started as friends and though we've always had a close bond, choosing to go through with a relationship had brought out the absolute worst in the both of us.

The ringing of my phone interrupted us. The incoming call was from Alaya.

"Yea Lay-Lay, what's up?"

"How'd it go?"

"How'd what go?"

"You told me you were taking Lem to her appointment today. Yaz, don't tell me you forgot about it."

"Lemme call you back."

Standing to my feet and looking at the time, Lem's appointment was scheduled for one o'clock, and I knew I had to be out judging by the time.

"Yo, you good, bro?"

"I gotta get outta here, dawg."

"Do what you gotta do."

෫෧

Arriving at Dr. Blanco's office, I see Lem emerging from the doors with Anadia. She'd caught a glimpse of me with a look of disapproval on her face.

"Hey, My Dear," I greeted Anadia, referring to the nickname I'd given her as a child. Sharing a hug, I kissed her cheek.

"I'll be in the car, Lem," she spoke, turning to me. "Baby boy, you're in for it."

Once she was out of sight, Lem folded her arms across her chest and waited for an exclamation.

"I asked you if you wanted to come with me, and what did you say?"

"Baby, I'm sorry. I lost track of time with Indie."

"Well, I called Anadia and asked her to come with me, so you can go back to Indie."

"Lem, come on."

"Come on what?" she repeated. "This is the second time you've missed an appointment, Ya. I'm not dealing with this or you right now, so move."

⚶

"You still mad at me?" Eating dinner in complete silence was all I needed to know that she wasn't pleased. Finishing up and waddling over to the sink with giving me the silent treatment, I nodded and finished my food.

"Lemme guess, his ass asking you for more fuckin' money? Hmm?"

"What's with this personal ass vendetta you got with him?" I questioned.

"Why the fuck is you always making excuses for a grown ass man, Yasir? You make all this money, yet this nigga only comes around when it's vital for him. Yo stupid ass be quick to jump the fence for him, but can't even do the simple gesture for attending a damn appointment you said you would come to for your damn woman and baby."

"Lem, you're upset about the appointment like you ain't gonna have no more!"

Before she could respond, my phone began ringing on the counter.

She grabbed it. Looking at it once, she pitched it at me as I dodged with widened eyes.

"What the fuck is wrong with you?"

"I'm tired of coming last to everyone, Yasir! If it's not your conniving ass mother or fuckin' Indie, then it's work!" she screamed.

"You're acting like this the end of the world over missing two appointments, Lem. You gotta understand, my life and the reason why I grind the way I do is to make living better for you, baby. I know I may travel a lot, and I may not be home as much as I need to, but if I had it any other way, you know I'd be here. Why you think I'm working so hard right now?"

"It's not just about the appointments. Don't you think this shit is scary for me? I don't have a mother. I don't have a big ass family like you do, and all I ask if for you to be there, baby. I can't do this on my own."

"Nobody said you had to. Where are you getting this from?"

"It's how I feel, Ya," she expressed. "It's what runs through my head every damn day when I'm in this big ass house on my own!"

"Lemy, I can't do a thing if I don't know what the problem is, and that's facts. So, when something is bothering you, instead of getting mad, pissed, and just holding the shit in, I'd really appreciate it if you just let me know from the jump."

This pregnancy was showing us both the true colors of change taking place, and I could tell Lem was terrified based off these few months. On numerous occasions, she's expressed how it's always been just her on her own and with that, I've promised to always be everything she needed.

"You gotta stop all this crying, man." I sighed smirking and pulling her into my chest. "It's gonna be alright, baby. Come on, stop crying."

The next day went smoother than the last. Throwing my all into work in order to be there for whenever the baby was born had come with some sacrifice. Every morning when I'd go into the office or have a trip, it was beginning harder and harder to leave her behind mainly because her doctor made it blatantly clear that traveling was out of the question as of now.

"I appreciate this, bro. I'ma pay you back, man—"

"It's cool, bruh. We family at the end of the day, and if I have it, then you have it too," I spoke to Indie.

Out the corner of my eye, I watched a woman emerged from an Uber and made her way towards Indie and me. Off the rip, I could tell she was a gutta bitch and judging by the natural scowl on her face, something about her had set off weird ass vibes. Light skinned with dark brown eyes along with fiery, dark red hair, she smiled as I noticed she had her eyes on Indie.

"Hey, baby." She smiled as the two shared a kiss. "What's up with you?"

"Look at you shining, just how I like it," he cheesed, completely smitten by whoever this broad was. "Oh baby, this is my brother, Yaz. Yaz this is my lady, Jhea."

Seeing her face before and not quite knowing from where I extended a hand as she shook with a smile.

"So, you're the best friend. Indie has told me so much about you. I sure do hope you don't mind sharing him."

"Oh nah, he's all yours. Sometimes I need to clean my hands with the nigga at times," I joked.

"Lemme chop it up with this nigga real quick, and we can head to the crib, baby."

"Nice to meet you, Yaz."

"You too."

Once she was out of sight, I widened my eyes as Indie started to laugh.

"You trying to fuckin' get on me and that's what the fuck yo ass been hiding at the house, nigga? The fuck did that happen?"

"I met her a while back, and shit just clicked. She's fine as fuck, right?"

"Stay outta trouble man, that's all I'ma say, but I got some shit to handle of my own, dawg. You take care of that debt though, real spill."

"I'm putting the shit together right now as we speak, love you, bro."

"Love you too, my nigga. Stay up."

Arriving to my next destination with my already tense mood being perplexed by guilt, I was being dead ass wrong. Removing my Cartier frames and stepping out of the vehicle, I gave Chev a nod as I entered. Renting out the location, wanting complete privacy, she sat sipping on her champagne while meeting my eyes.

"I was starting to think you wouldn't show."

"If I didn't, you would've kept going, so I'm ending this shit now."

An ex-flame was an ex-flame for a reason. Brielle and I had a history that had run deeper than any bond I've shared with a woman. My love for Lem was undeniable and naturally brought about by us being from different aspects of life, which had caused everything to make sense. With Brielle, when we were good, we were damn good, and when we were bad, shit was destructive.

Having not seen her for years now, I honestly didn't know how to feel. Part of my reason for showing up was to put an end to the bull-shit, especially since I was in such a comfortable space within my life right now.

"Does she know you here?"

"What's the point of all this shit, man? Why are you going through my moms and all this fuck shit? What the fuck you got up your sleeve, Bri?"

"Your mom told me about the baby. I'm hurt that I didn't hear it from you."

"What the hell I look like telling my ex about my child?"

"This child could very well not be yours, Yasir. Don't be fuckin' stupid."

"You'on know shit, and if you think sticking close to my mama is gonna someway make me come back, you're sadly mistaken. What we had is done. What are you holding onto?"

"If you were so done, then why'd you come here? If you were so done, why have you been replying to my texts and my calls?" Bri asked. "You're putting on this façade like you don't care about me when we both know I was everything to you. She doesn't know shit about you nor has she ever seen you at your worse."

"This was a mistake," I spoke, standing to my feet. "Stay the fuck away from me and stay even further away from my family."

"That's a threat?"

"Nah, it's a warning. The next time I won't be as lenient, now that...that's a promise."

LEMY

"I really wish you'd stop pouting, bitch," Milan fussed. "God, you're putting me through it, and my ass is not even fuckin' pregnant."

"She's upset because she and Yaz are into it again. They'll be back all over each other by tomorrow," Alaya adds. "I had to learn that hard way not to take it seriously with these two. The only thing it'll do is cause you the headache as well."

"Ya know, I never really remember asking either one of you bitches for an opinion."

"How'd the appointment go?"

"Well as of now, I gotta have a C-section, but that could change. Per usual, my blood pressure was pretty high, so if nothing changes, I'll be on bed rest until I deliver."

"Yaz was saying you two were going to tour a hospital. How'd that go?"

"I wasn't feeling it. I don't wanna be somewhere giving birth where I can't even enjoy the excitement that comes along with it just being me, him, and our baby. As bad as it is, I already gotta deal with his rep and all this other shit. I think I want a home birth because doing it in a hospital is currently outta the question."

"Do what you feel is best, hell I'ma be Teedie until Trevan and I ready to have a few." Alaya laughed.

"Uh, same," Milan added.

Friendships were seldom, but with meeting Alaya, our bond was set in stone, and I've also formed a close relationship with Anadia, Alaya's mother. The Cosart family was close-knit, despite Dara's having two children with two different women and as weird as it seemed, Anadia and Gen B were close.

With the stress that's come along with my mother-in-law wanting to dictate every single thing her son does, I took more of a liking to Anadia. She remained true to the nickname Yaz had given her because she was a dear gentle soul. She'd accepted me with open arms, and in my eyes, she is who I wanted to be at my side as that mother figure when I gave birth.

Finishing off my food and reaching over into Milan's plate, she slapped my hand away, causing Alaya to laugh with shaking her head.

"You sure it's just one in there?"

"Oh yes, it's only one."

"Miss Lemy," Chev announced, clearing his throat. "Pardon my interrupting, but Sir sent me."

"Is everything okay?"

"Yes ma'am, he just asked I retrieve you immediately."

Bidding a farewell to my girls, I followed Chev as we left the private dining area of the restaurant and to the SUV parked outside. He opened the door as I climbed inside where Yaz sat in deep thought, looking irritated as I removed my shades.

"What's going on?" I inquired.

"A lot of shit been happening and we ain't been in the best space, so I felt like we needed a getaway. I had My Dear pack you some things and we're headed to the jet right now."

"Dr. Mason said it was okay?"

"Yea, I spoke to her this morning."

For as long as I've been with this nigga, I knew when some shit was bothering him because he was vague and damn near cold. Figuring this probably was just something miniscule I dropped it but would soon be bringing it up once again and at a much better time.

Arriving in Calabasas, where the weather was much beautiful than in Louisiana, we were unpacking in the private vacation home. According to him, he hadn't been to this place in almost two years, and it was where he often retreated when he needed a release from his work life, family and whatever else was bothering him at the moment.

6lack's "Loaded Gun" played from the sound bar erupting throughout our bedroom as the heat between us intensified immensely. Laid on my side, he delivered sweet kisses trailing down my spine as I turned my head, kissing him sloppily as he penetrated my soaked folds while I gripped onto the sheets.

No shit, I treat my dick just like a loaded gun.

The lyrics alone igniting him as he sucked on my neck and held my thigh. The painful pleasure bringing tears to my eyes as I moaned continuously, my voice cracking. His hunger and appetite, along with whatever had him stressed, was currently being taken out on me as I enjoyed every second.

Pulling out as I laid onto my back, he pressed his lips to mine and pried my legs open. With accurate precision, his tongue darted continuously onto my throbbing clitoris. Wanting so terribly to push him away, I endured the delivering of his head game as he ate it up as if were his last possible meal.

"Ya," I breathed out, biting my lip.

My eyes rolled into the back of my head as he gripped my thighs, coming up and licking his lips. Bringing his face to mine, I tasted myself on his lips, the simple gesture turning me on even more. His tongue delved into my mouth as he held my throat while rubbing his fingers between my other set of lips. Bringing his fingers to his mouth, I turned over on all fours as he rammed inside while I held onto the headboard.

"Throw that shit back," he demanded in a low, sexy tone.

Delivering a slap to my ass, I followed his commands feeling my juices trailing down my legs. Thoroughly exhausted and deepening my arch, an overwhelming emotion starting in the pit of my stomach had erupted as my legs began to shake. The pleasurable euphoria was taking me by storm as he pushed himself deeper and holding it there as I climaxed.

Foolishly knowing it didn't end there, he pulled me into him as my back collided with his chest. Moving up and down onto his shaft with the little energy I had left, unable to contain my moans, I screamed and squeezed his hand as he sucked onto my neck. Starting up again as we moved against each other in a sexually infused symphony, he hissed and cupped my breasts.

"Fuck, you 'bouta make me nut!"

His body tensed immediately, and for a second time, I exploded as he followed right behind me. Still inside of me as my chest heaved up and down, I twisted my neck as we shared another sloppy kiss. Smiling against my lips, he moved my hair from my face as we laid in the spooning position.

With our hands resting on my stomach, he chuckled and began to rub as he kissed my neck again.

"Remember how I always told you I'd be real with you from the jump, no matter how fucked up a situation was?"

Frowning and turning around to face him, while touching his face, I started to see a look of uncertainty in his eyes.

"What'd you do?"

"Brielle been reaching out to me talking crazy shit, and I went to see her to put a stop to it," he expressed. Anger began to reach its peak as I smacked my lips.

"So, your attempt to fuck me and take me outta town was in an effort to throw me off so that I wouldn't punch you in your shit over this?"

"I didn't do anything wrong."

Climbing out of bed and no longer wanting to hear the rest of this conversation. He started to sigh as I pulled on a shirt. Turning off the music and leaving the room to go into the bathroom, I started my shower water as I turned around to see him headed towards me.

"Just listen and stop running away from me. There's a reason I'm telling you all of this. Just calm down."

"What?"

"Mama told her how she felt about the baby and right now, ain't nobody about to badmouth my child behind my back. So, how you wanna go about this?"

"This is all you. She's your mother, not mine. But as of now, I don't want her around my baby."

"Not a problem, anything else?" Seeing how serious this matter bothered him, I'd calmed down because he didn't even have to tell me the truth.

"Thank you for telling me."

"I meant what I said," he spoke, kissing my forehead. "Nothing or nobody is coming between what we have, and that's a promise."

As the month neared its end, things proceeded to get better between us. Taking some time from work and spending much more time at home as we prepped for the baby, right now we were going over financials for this grand ass gender reveal/baby shower Milan and Alaya were throwing for us.

"Fuckin' three racks for a cake?" Yaz fussed, shaking his head. "Oh, hell fuckin' no."

"Baby, stop," I laughed. "Lani, can we just find a cheaper cake before he fuckin' strokes out?"

"Yea, we can find another one. What's our budget, Yaz?"

Meeting my stare as I blinked, I allowed my mink eyelash extensions to get through to him as he looked unfazed.

"We will um, give y'all some time to think things over. The party planner will be here in fifteen, so don't take too long," Alaya warned. Left alone, I turned to him as he grabbed my hand and kissed it.

"I wanted to run something by you."

"What is it?"

"Indie coming to the baby shower, him and his girl. How would you feel about that?"

"Honestly, I'm not a big fan of him, and I get he's your friend, but I want this shower to be special for both of us."

"So that's a no?"

"It's a maybe, all depending on how I feel. Why are you always so good to him?"

"Because honestly, I'm all he has," he shrugged. "You'on know him like I do, and I don't expect for you to, but I kinda feel like I gotta be there for him."

"You have a good heart, Poppa," I spoke sweetly. "I just don't want anybody taking advantage of that or all that you've worked so hard for. That's all."

"I'm a big boy, baby I can handle it. I do appreciate the concern, but I got this. Let ya man handle it, and you just don't worry your pretty little head, a'ight?"

"Yes, daddy."

Chapter Four

YAZ

"How's the baby shower and reveal planning going?"

"Lem's friend and Alaya are planning it with the planner, so we going somewhere. Look, mama, can we talk real quick? It's just something I need to get off my chest."

"I raised you to always speak up," she stated, joining me at the table. "What's on your mind?"

"I spoke with Brielle, and she told me some things that didn't quite sit well with me. I understand you want to protect me, but with all due respect mama, I'm a grown man, and I don't need you to be moving a certain way when it comes down to my family. I love Lem, and I'm going to marry her. I'm sorry you don't agree with that, but why did you feel it comfortable to mouth off to my ex?"

"You could've lost your damn life last year, and everybody knows it is because of that girl, now don't you sit here talking to me like—"

"See, that's what I'm talking about," I stressed. "This is not about you, mama. This shit is about me."

"When will you open up your fuckin' eyes, Yasir?" she fussed, smacking her lips and shaking her head. "I refuse to sit around pretending as if this girl is something special because she isn't. She's a leech, and you will soon see what the hell I mean. You need to have a blood test done."

"We've always had a good relationship, and no matter how much you meddled in my life, I always stood by your side through the good and bad. So, why is it so hard for you to accept her? I don't need to do a damn thing because I know the truth. If you don't wanna deal with either one of them, then don't. I'm not begging or asking you to."

"As a matter of fact, get on outta my house with all this shit! How dare you turn your back on your mother? When your stupid ass father was out doing God knows what, who was there making sure you were in the best schools, greatest programs, and everything else your ungrateful ass was in? Huh!"

"I didn't ask you for none of that! You had the chance to leave pops. You're the one who stayed! Don't take that shit out on me!"

"I will do whatever the hell I want, and you wanna know why, because I sacrificed all those things to assure you didn't make no stupid ass decisions like this, Yasir! Look at you!" she shouted. "I am extremely disappointed in you!"

"Where's your loyalty? To me, as your son!"

"That loyalty went out the door as soon as you fucked that whore! How could you be so stupid?"

"Well, you feel that way, mama. Ain't nobody stopping you, but keep that same energy when my baby gets here because with the way it's looking...the only grandmother she or he will acknowledge is Anadia," I fumed, standing to my feet. "I love you."

Turning my back as she continued to shout all painful things possible, I couldn't believe she'd had gone to extreme heights all because of her dislike for Lem. No matter what, I've always remained in mama's corner, even if I didn't always agree with some of the shit she's done.

I've battled so much within myself daily, and sadly, this would be another instance when I'd have to pretend as if the shit didn't bother me. Carrying so much weight on my shoulders was often pushed in the back of my mind with work, burying my emotions in a bottle, or simply just sticking my dick in any woman with a wet pussy.

Refusing to cry, only because I was taught to show no emotion whatsoever, I silently climbed into the SUV as Chev entered, and we drove off.

"Sir?"

"Take me home, man."

"Very well, sir."

Arriving at our home, the aroma of cooking stemming from the kitchen had managed to capture my attention. Entering the kitchen, I watched Lem stood at the stove with her stomach on display as she turned to me with a smile.

"Hey, baby," she cheesed. "How was work?"

"Straight."

Opening the cabinet to grab my Crown Royal bottle with a shot glass, I poured up and took it to the head, soon refilling the shot glass and throwing it back once again. The alcohol traveled down my throat, creating a burning sensation as I placed it back into the cabinet.

"Whoa?" she frowned, walking over as she pecked my lips. "Baby, talk to me. What happened?"

"Nothing, I'm good. Lemme know when the food finished, a'ight?"

"Yasir."

"What, Lem?" I stressed. "It's been a long day. I just need a minute. A'ight?"

"Alright, fine."

Anything remotely possible to my being too snippy would cause her to burst out in tears or cuss me out, which is why I kept it short and sweet. Entering our bedroom and removing my clothing, I switched to my usual Nike sweats. Shirtless, I entered the closet and grabbed my keepsake box as I traveled outside to the balcony.

Filled with weed, rolling papers, cigars, and a blade, I picked up the pill bottle, which I hadn't touched in years. Stemming from an injury I suffered in college when I played ball, every now and then I'd suffer from some nerve pain whereas my doctor at the time had prescribed morphine. Taking one of the pills from the bottle and grinding it down to a powder, I sprinkled it into my blunt and proceeded to roll. Keeping my eye on the door, standing up to lock it, I finished up and lit up while inhaling.

As I engulfed the concoction so effortlessly, the stress literally melted away with every pull I took from the blunt. Over and over again, I continued this until the events, which had taken place earlier, were now a thing of the past.

§⋅

"You look tired as shit, bro," Indie commented.

"Damn nigga, can I just come to see yo ass without all the extra bullshit?"

After the last loan I'd given Indie to get him out of yet another debt, he'd moved in with his current fling, Jhea. Still not knowing how to feel about this relationship he shared with this woman, I just remained in his corner.

The two resided together, so after working out at the crib, I stepped out to get some fresh air, and I decided to visit him. Creating a rotation between us both, J. Cole's hits played from his flat screen as we sat just touching base with the shit taking place in our lives.

"Yaz, hi I didn't know you were," Jhea greets. She was dressed in a tube top, showcasing her flat stomach and navel piercing matched with the jeans, which gave her great justice to her flawless frame filling them out amazingly well.

"What's up?"

"Baby, I'm headed out for a minute to get my nails done. I'll see you later, okay?"

"Be careful."

"I will. See you guys later."

Not wanting to stare at my man's property, once she was out of sight, Indie laughed as I shook my head.

"Dawg, so this shit serious, huh?"

"You see it, don't you? Moneyman Cosart, the only nigga who can fall in love, huh?"

"Man lemme take my ass home to my woman before you get my ass killed."

§⋅

"You're done being an ass," Lem commented as I wrapped my arms around her from behind. Ignoring her statement, I kissed her jaw and pecked her lips as she placed my dinner in front of me.

"So it's cool for you to be in your moods, but I can't?"

"I'm pregnant with your child, so that explains my craziness. Alaya told me you're not speaking to Gen B. What happened?"

"This blackened salmon is good as a bitch. You did something new to it?"

"Nigga, get fucked up."

"To be honest, I don't wanna get into all that right now, bae."

"Okay, fine with me. Well, I'll leave you to it." She yawned. "I'm going to soak because my back is killing me. I love you."

"I love you too, baby."

Chapter Five

LEMY

"Okay, on the count of three, you two!"

"One, two, three!"

Using my knife to cut into the cake as my heart thumped out of my chest, cameras flashed from all different angles as Yaz eagerly held my waist. Anticipating the reveal of our baby, I cut a slice to see not a speck of pink or blue.

"What the fuck!?"

"Wait, this not the real one?" Yaz questioned.

Everyone had come out to celebrate the arrival of Baby Cosart as well as the gender being revealed. Dressed to impress, Yaz and I matched eloquently prior to the festivities as well as everyone else taking part as well. Joined together with our friends, family, and some of his colleagues from work as well as my old coworkers, I wanted nothing but to be surrounded by all good vibes on this special day.

"Alaya, where's the real one!"

"I have no idea what you're talking about," she sang.

Completely frustrated at this point and my emotions taking a toll, I cried into Yaz's chest as he held me.

"See what you did to my baby, man," he fussed.

"Aw, we didn't mean to make you cry, Lem," Milan whined. "Okay, y'all forreal I can't take seeing her like this."

"Okay, alright. Damn, I just wanted to have some fun."

Yaz wiped my eyes, carefully not wanting to smear my mascara as he kissed my jaw.

"Alright, everyone if you'll turn your attention to the screen, please!" Milan announced. "Lem and Yaz, you two make your way to the stage."

"If you bitches are playing my ass again, I don't wanna fuckin' go!"

My outburst caused everyone to laugh as Yaz held my hand as we made our way to the stage. Turning our attention to the screen, a video started with the camera placed on me at one of our appointments. My heart warmed at the sight as Yaz's face had come into view as I smiled, the sound of our baby's heartbeat erupting.

Small snippets throughout the pregnancy were shown and even some pictures from some trips we've taken together. The majority of them were done on the sneak side, which made them seem more beautiful. Tearing up, some people cooed as I fanned my eyes watching as Yaz's face had come into view.

"The gift of life is an amazing thing, man. I can't even put it into words. To my child, you are so loved by everyone who's awaiting your arrival. Your mommy and I are so excited to meet you. Daddy's anxious, but I know once I lay eyes on your face, all of my worries will be a thing of the past."

A montage of more video clips was shown with melodic music playing in the background as the gesture caused the tears to flow rapidly. Unable to contain my emotions, one of the last pictures was from our babymoon where he'd taken a picture without my knowledge as I was walking on the beach.

Lastly, a message was posted, which caused me to frown.

"Lem and Yaz, read it aloud."

"No, fuck y'all," I fussed through my tears, causing everyone to laugh.

"Come on, baby. Don't be mean," Yaz laughed.

"Okay, let's do it."

"In mommy's belly, I will grow. Ten tiny fingers, ten tiny toes, some don't know what my gender will be, although you might already see.

Guess if I'm a girl or boy, I'm sure either way, you will jump for joy.
Read this riddle with great care. Look really close. It's really there," we
recited in unison.

"What the fuck?" Yaz fussed. "Okay, who's responsible for this?"

"I'm with my man on this one. I don't get it."

"You have to look closely!" someone yelled.

"I am looking, and I don't see shit!" I snapped, laughing. "Somebody help me."

"Nope, you gotta get this one on your own," Milan added. "Nobody
say anything, Yaz and Lem will have to guess!"

"Bullshit," I fussed into the mic. "Y'all I don't get it."

"Man, y'all are stressing her out!" Yaz joked. "Don't you know you
can't stress out a pregnant lady!"

"Okay, okay you guys since they refuse to partake. We'll go ahead
with it. Cue the confetti!"

In an instant, the confetti had popped as pink sprinkled every-
where. Screaming with excitement, we shared a hug as Yaz rocked me
back and forth as Stevie Wonder's "Isn't She Lovely" began to play.

"Wait, I still don't get the riddle," I complained.

"Vertically, the first letters of each phrase spells out It's A Girl,"
Milan announced.

Night had fallen, and the day's events replayed themselves in my mind
as I looked around seeing how blessed this child was already. The room
we'd cleared out and chosen for the nursery was already filled with shit
from everyone. We'd received so much that it had to be put into one of
the extra rooms where we'd sort through everything once Yaz decided
to take his leave from work.

Exiting the room, only to hear voices, I stopped in my tracks.
Hearing Indie talking, my skin began to crawl. Truly not wanting to
do with this snake, I tried my damn hardest to get Yaz to understand
my utter dislike for him, but it literally went in one ear and out the
other.

Not in the mood for even looking at this fuck nigga's face, I traveled to our bedroom and stripped down to my usual large t-shirt while climbing into bed.

Loud ass music coming from outside had managed to catch my attention as I got right back out of bed to look out the window. Unable to make out who was pushing the all-new looking Porsche, I left well enough alone and got back in the bed.

Some odd minutes later, Yaz entered with his eyes glossy, reddened, and low. Already knowing he probably smoked with Indie, he'd gotten into bed and tried to kiss me as I backed away.

"You smell like that shit, get back."

"Here you go." He sighed. "What I do?"

"Who was that outside?"

"Indie's bitch, some chick he with."

"She must got money. The bitch is pushing a Porsche. Fuck type of shit they got going on?"

"I don't know and don't fuckin' care," he replied, rubbing my stomach. "Daddy's Dudi. Didn't I tell you?"

"You need to lay off the weed. It's getting outta control. This is the third time this week."

"It's just a lil' weed. That shit ain't never hurt nobody. Why you tripping?"

Before I could answer, his work phone began going off with an incoming call from Lydia, his head of information technology.

"Talk to me."

"Sir, I'm so sorry to disturb you at this late hour, but there's been a breach at HQ. I'm sending you images from security right now."

Grabbing the MacBook from my lap, he quickly logged into it, and the pictures had popped up as he ran his hands over his face.

"Any word on what they were looking for?"

"It's a bit unclear as of now, but we're working on it. The assailant was last seen on the floor of your office, but no entry. Once we discover the motive behind the breach, we'll inform you, but we do believe whoever it is was not working alone."

"Initiate the emergency firewalls and wipe everything important you can find off the servers."

"Are you sure, sir?"

"Yes, it's completely fine. I did a backup last month. I'll just handle everything when I make it in the morning. Be sure to have Becca schedule a meeting first thing too so that we can alert everybody."

"I'm on it, and once again sir, I'm very sorry for interrupting you."

"It's okay, no worries. Thank you."

"You're welcome, you have a nice night, sir."

"You too."

Turning our attention to the screen of my MacBook, the assailant was masked and in black as he slammed it shut. Climbing over to massage his shoulders, he had calmed down as I kissed the nape of his neck.

Wrapping my arms around him, he turned his head as we shared a kiss. Grabbing my hand, I got out of bed as he sat on the edge placing his hands on my waist and kissing my stomach as we remained in the same position.

§●

"Just please come keep me company before I blow this bitch up, I don't even know why he agreed to travel to fuckin' Manhattan knowing that I can have this baby any day now."

"You're only thirty-six weeks Lem, relax with the unneeded dramatics. Milan and I will be there in a bit, plus mama gave me those crawfish pies you asked for."

"Yes, because I'm starving. Hurry up."

"Bye, fool."

Practically in the homestretch of this pregnancy, Yaz and I had ultimately decided to take the home birth route since I was cleared for no longer needing a C-section. Luckily Dr. Mason had referred us to Chandler Brooks, a colleague of hers and current midwife while I'd stumbled upon Reeba Jenkins, who would serve as the doula.

The birth plan was laid out to perfection. The only thing we were waiting on was baby girl's arrival. Yaz had an emergency meeting with some important people, which had caused him to be away for a few days. Today marked day three and he'd be returning sometime tonight or tomorrow morning.

The sudden ringing of the doorbell had started. As I went to grab the door, all into my phone, I opened it to reveal Indie. An immediate scowl crept onto my face as he pushed his way inside.

"You need to get the fuck out."

"Come on now, Lem. Don't be so quick to turn the blind eye," he spoke, glancing around. "After all, you have hit the jackpot."

"I'm calling Yasir." Knocking the phone from my hands and onto the floor with this look in his eyes, Indie was standing inches away from me as he shook his head.

"You think you this shit made, don't you? It'd be such a shame to see everything you took be taken away from you."

"Get your fuckin' hands off me—"

"Bitch, I'll fuckin' kill you right here, right now. Shut the fuck up!"

"I can't see how my nigga could be so blind to the fact that you're a fuckin' jealous ass bastard who cannot stand to see him fuckin' happy." Grabbing onto my arm, squeezing tightly as he forcefully pushed me into the wall as I yanked away from him. "Admit it. He has everything you wish you had."

"What? You?" He laughed, chuckling as he licked his lips. "Nah baby, been there, done that and had that. Did you seem to forget?" Running his finger across my face, I slapped them away as he forcefully grabbed my throat.

"What the fuck do you want?"

"You'll see." He nodded, kissing his lips at me. Pushing him off, he winked at me and made his exit. Feeling dirty, I locked the door and rushed to the nearest bathroom, throwing up profusely.

Once again, just when everything was starting to flow smoothly, my past was coming back to haunt me in more ways than one. Pulling myself up from the floor, I flushed and went to look at my reflection in the mirror, becoming proud of how much I've changed. This time around, I refused to allow my past to threaten my future, and I'll be damned if I allowed one foolish decision to fuck up my entirety.

Chapter Six

YAZ

"How is she doing?"

"She's in a lot of pain, but she's okay," Alaya stated. "We're all here, so she's in good hands. How far out are you?"

"About fifteen minutes away, what's the update?"

"Her contractions are every fifteen to twenty minutes," she spoke over Lem's screaming. "Get here now, Yaz. She needs you."

"I'm coming. Let her know I'm headed to her right now."

"I will and be careful, bro."

In the middle of what would have been one of the most significant meetings of my life, I'd received the call from Alaya that Lem's water broke. Not knowing I would be up against the hands of time when I agreed to schedule the trip to Manhattan, I was willingly battling all odds possible to get home to be at my woman's side.

Baby girl wasn't expected for another few weeks, but before leaving Lem complained about discomfort. Though it was, in fact, a risk, this child was on her own time and ready to make her debut.

"What's our status, Chev?"

"We're moving now, sir."

Courtesy of NOPD, they'd owed me a valid favor, so I'd made the call for a police escort from my jet to the house. Traffic was at a bit of a

standstill with it being lunchtime, but as we sped through, I antici-
pated what is said to be the most joyous time of a man's life.

"Approaching now, sir," Chev announced.

Zooming through the gates, I unbuckled my seatbelt and removed
my blazer. Once the vehicle had come to a stop, I'd sprinted out the
car and to the door. Upon entering, Lem's screams erupted from the
bedroom.

Rushing to her side, I'd entered our bedroom where she was
hunched over with tears streaming down her face.

"Baby, you're here."

"I'm here. You thought you were doing this shit without me, girl?"

Shaking her head no, I pressed my lips to hers and wiped away her
tears.

Labor had picked up progressively, and although she was taking it
like a champ, I could see the immediate exhaustion taking place.
Chandler and Reeba had filled the birthing tub with warm water as
Lem and I had gotten inside.

"Does it feels good, Lem?" Anadia questioned.

Lem nodded while holding my hands as Chandler checked her to
see how far she'd dilated. To keep from screaming, Reeba was
guiding her on her breathing. With her back against my chest, she
tensed up and frowned as I kissed her neck as she squeezed my
hand.

"Ouch, ouch," she whined.

"She's eight centimeters. She's almost there," Chandler announced.

"You're doing so good, baby. Poppa's so proud of you," I coached.
"It'll be all over soon. Just a lil' bit longer and she'll be here. Our baby
girl is gonna be so beautiful, I already know it. She's so blessed to have
you, baby."

"A little longer," she repeated, her eyes closed. "I can do this, right?"

"You are doing it, Lemy."

"I can do this," she nodded, crying. "Ouu, I can do this."

ૐ

Nine hours had passed, and we were now at the finish line awaiting our most precious gift. Alaya, Milan, Pops, Trevan, and My Dear were all awaiting downstairs.

Holding her hands as she squeezed it to let me know another contraction had started. No longer screaming, she frowned and breathed through it as she whimpered. My heart ached terribly seeing her undergo so much pain. I wanted so terribly to switch positions with her as tears continued to slip from her eyes, but her strength was nothing short of beauty in my eyes.

"Take me out of the water. I wanna get out."

Rushing to her side, we migrated to the bed, and in the midst of walking, she caught another contraction as she cried out.

"Breathe Lemy, just like we've been practicing. It's okay. You're doing good."

"I just need a fuckin' minute, alright!" she screamed. "Just...gimme a minute."

Finally moving to the bed, she laid on her side and started to sob. Feeling practically useless, I rubbed her lower back as she calmed down.

"I just want her out," she wailed.

"Baby, I'm going down to let everybody—"

"Don't you fuckin' leave me, Yaz. Please, don't. I need you!"

Deciding on staying at her side, she'd practiced pushing and judging by how well she was doing Chandler said the baby would be present within the next thirty minutes. Unable to push comfortably while lying on her back, Alaya had entered with the camera as we all waited for another contraction to ensue.

"On your mark, Lemy. Whenever you're ready," Reeba instructed.

Nodding as I continued to rub her lower back, she got down on all fours and started to push as Chandler began a countdown from ten to one. Screaming out breathlessly, my heart anxiously thumped out of my chest as she squeezed my free hand as my eyes widened at how strong she was holding onto me.

She let out a gut-wrenching scream after going right back into it as she was instructed, and as I looked down, our baby girl was in Chandler's arms. Overjoyed tears clouded my vision as our baby girl's small cries filled the room.

"Congratulations, it's a girl!"

Witnessing this miracle, our emotions were high. I cut the umbilical cord as I was instructed and our baby girl was placed into Lem's arms. As soon as she entered her mother's arms, her crying had ceased, and that alone had to be the most touching thing I'd ever witnessed. In the moment, I realized this was really what it was all about. I wanted nothing more than to be a better man for them both.

As the weeks progressed, reality had hit with a force like no other, and everything had immediately kicked into high gear, putting this all into a much bigger perspective for both of us. As new parents, we struggled with learning all that we needed to, and although it was indeed tough, I wouldn't have had it any other way.

We'd decided on naming her Yara Aneema Cosart, her first name meaning, someone close to your heart, and her middle name paying homage to Lemy's sister which was the perfect name for our little, precious princess who currently had all of her daddy's love.

I saw not a single flaw within her. Blessed with a caramel tone similar to mine, she also had brown eyes, which often changed to a light tint of brown and sometimes darker, which is something Lem says her sister eyes would often do. Her coal colored hair along with those little lips similar to mine and a nose like her mother was all I needed that there was no doubt in my mind that this little girl had belonged to me.

"Daddy loves you so much, Dudi," I whispered. "I know this is still kinda new to your mommy and me, but we're giving it all we got. I love you so much, baby and seeing the joy you've brought your mommy...it warms my heart. Your life is going to be so full of joy and happy moments. We honestly can't wait. Everything is yours, my love. The sky's the limit for you. I'll do whatever you need and make sure to be the best father I can be for you. I love you, baby girl."

"You're going to have her completely spoiled," Lemy spoke, observing us from the door. "Looks like mommy's got some competition."

"Listen to you. Did you get enough rest?"

"No, not quite. I can't sleep until I know she's gotten enough." She yawned. "Will you please come to bed?"

"I'll be there in a minute. Make it warm for me, a'ight?" She nodded as we shared a kiss then left the nursery as Yara's eyes started to grow heavy. Sucking on her bottle containing Lem's breast milk, she continued as I removed the bottle from her mouth and burped her.

After a proper burping and cleaning her up, I laid her into her crib and retreated to our bedroom where Lem stood admiring her frame in the full-length mirror.

"No need to stop on my account, beautiful. What's wrong?"

"Just looking at what used to fuckin' be." She sighed. "How'd she do?"

"She had her last bottle for the night, and she's out. I made sure to cut on the baby monitor too," I spoke, patting the empty side of the bed. "You gonna keep me waiting or what?"

Like any woman who'd just given birth, postpartum had done some damage, and I was there to pick up the pieces. Whether it was her crying fits, her not being used to the way her body now looked, or simply just being overwhelmed, it'd unknowingly brought us closer as a couple.

All of her insecurities were on full display, and her emotions wouldn't allow that wall to be built up like she'd usually have to fall back on. Everything was now out in the open and honestly seeing her in this new light was the sight that I'd been dying to see because it is what made her the most beautiful in my eyes.

"I'ma miss the fuck outta you when you go back to work." She pouted. "It's so nice having you here at all times to help with Yara and even trying to cook and shit. Now it's just gonna be Yara and me. That's crazy."

"You're strong enough to handle it. I don't doubt that you'll succeed, and you know I'm always a call away. Then My Dear, Laya, and Milan are gonna be here."

"Yea baby, but they're not you. I could have all the help in the world possible, but that doesn't even amount up to all that you do for us. I'll just have to adjust, that's all."

"I know you been getting better with your depression and all. How are you feeling now?"

"Every now and then, I'll have a moment." She shrugged, leaning into my chest. "But it's much easier in a way. I just hate being locked in this big ass house, sometimes. It's the summertime, and I'm inside with a newborn. It's a lot to take in."

"That's the way life is maw. You gotta get with it. Think about it. Around this time next year, we'll be married and laughing at this with a one a year old, so it's just going to take some well needed time."

"I just wanna be able to be transparent with us being able to communicate on certain things. But, I want you to promise me if you're getting in any way overwhelmed you'd let me know."

"You got my word. Man, what I told you?"

"I know. I'm just so used to one thing," she responded with a yawn. "Thank you for never giving up on me, Yasir. I'm serious. It really means a lot to me."

"As I said before, I'm here every step of the way. You'll always have me. Forever and I mean that."

Chapter Seven

LEMY

"I fuckin' said no Yasir, just drop it."

"Now if I would've done the shit behind your back, it would've been the end of the damn world. Why are you so hostile?"

With welcoming our new bundle, it was almost as if more drama had unraveled from out of nowhere. Not only did I have to deal with everyone begging my ass to allow Gen B to meet Yara, but I also had Yaz in my ear on Indie being her godfather, which I refused. Deep down I wanted to tell him about the history behind why I held such an intense hatred for Indie, but we were doing so good right now, and I didn't want my past problems fucking up yet another good thing.

"Because I got enough shit on my plate as is, why can't you understand that?" I belted, igniting Yara's crying.

Completely frustrated by damn near everyone who'd come in an arm's reach, I knew this postpartum was basically playing my ass like a fiddle. Angry tears filled my eyes as I entered her nursery. Scooping her up and shushing her only caused her to cry even more.

"I'm so sorry that I'm all over the place baby, but you have to cut your mommy some slack. Okay?" Speaking as if she understood, I was clueless and simply rocked her until she settled down.

If I could describe my emotions since giving birth, I would have to say it was similar to being stranded in the middle of a lake and drowning while no one is able to neither hear nor see how you're suffering. No matter how much Yaz would help out or even the girls, it was never adequately enough because I couldn't help but feel as if I were doing this all wrong.

Observing her flawless features as she innocently sucked from my breasts, her light colored eyes were getting lower. Never really knowing a love like this could exist, I was blown away at how great of a hold she'd had on my heart.

I wanted to be the best woman possible, all for her sake. Nothing else mattered, and I didn't care about anything in this world. All that was on my mind was making this life a perfect one, all for her.

At only three and a half weeks, I saw so much of Neema within her. Just the thought of knowing she had two guardian angels at her side at all times made it much easier to deal with their absence of not being physically here.

Sensing a presence, I'd glanced up to see Yaz standing in the doorway watching us as I continued to focus on her.

"All she wanted was her mommy," he whispered, kneeling beside us. "You okay?"

"I will be."

"I don't mean to upset you," he expressed, caressing my face. "I may not exactly know how tough it is, but I just want you to know I'm here, Lemy, always."

"I know and I just..."

"You'on have to get into all that if you don't want to, baby, I understand. I know it's been irritating as fuck with everybody beating down your back with all this and I'ma put a stop to all that."

"I don't expect for you to shun out your mother, Ya."

"She shunned herself, so all my cards are dealt. I don't want anybody around my daughter whose gonna bring about bad vibes. You and her both are my everything, and I'll be damned if anybody ruins that."

"Okay, it's your call."

Having not been outside the house in weeks after giving birth, I damn near shed tears once Milan and Alaya hit me up saying we were having a lunch date. Trusting Yaz with Yara, I was still a bit nervous with this being the very first time I'd left her side since she's been born. She would forever be in good hands with her dad, but it just felt unusual.

"You sure you're gonna be okay here? I can stay, Ya. It's fine."

"Go out and enjoy yourself, I already told you she's in good hands, and if I get my hands tied, I'm calling My Dear. Go have a good time, baby. You deserve it."

"You've been complaining about a headache though."

"A lil' headache ain't gonna do me nothing."

"You sure?"

"Halima, go 'head."

Sighing and nodding as I grabbed my things, he joined me at my side as he bent down, pressing his lips to mine while grasping my ass. Giggling against his lips and pecking them once more, he delivered a slap as he held my face.

"I love you and be careful, a'ight?"

"I love you too."

Pouting and making my way over to Yara, she was sleeping in her swing. I kissed her forehead. Wanting so terribly to wake her up, my emotions began to take over. As I wiped away my tears, she squirmed. I was about to pick her up until Yaz stopped me.

"Uh-uh. Nah, get back and leave her alone," he fussed. "I know yo ass ain't crying, dawg."

"Shut the fuck up. I didn't know it was gonna be this hard."

Pinching the bridge of his nose, he stumbled back a little as I frowned.

"Baby?"

"I'm straight. It's fine."

"You don't look straight or fine. Yasir, you're sweating."

"You're overreacting," he fussed, waving it off. "Stop and get on outta here."

Retreating to the bathroom, I still didn't believe he was okay. Following my better judgment, I decided on calling Milan.

"We're outside."

"I'm not coming anymore. Something is up with Yaz, and he's lying to me. Y'all can go ahead without me."

"You sure?"

Hearing what sounded like a bunch of shit falling to the floor, my phone dropped from my hands as I rushed into the bathroom and pushed the door open to see him on the floor, unresponsive.

"Baby!" I screamed, rushing to his side. "Yasir, baby, can you hear me?"

"What happened?" he mumbled.

"Stay right here," I fussed, rushing to get my phone. "Milan, please get in here. I need someone to watch Yara while I take him to the hospital."

"Is he okay?"

"I don't fuckin' know. He passed out! Look, just use the spare and get in here."

Rushing to his side and hanging up, I helped him up. I struggled being that he was half my size. Completely disoriented, I used all of my strength to bring him to the garage as I placed him inside the Audi. Putting his seatbelt on and unable to make out what he was saying, he opened the door and began throwing up.

Running back into the house to grab my purse and his wallet, I rushed back out and climbed into the car as we started on our way to the hospital.

§

Sitting in the waiting room waiting to see what the problem might have been, I started pacing and checking the time on my Apple Watch. My phone vibrated with an incoming call from Milan as I answered.

"Hey girl, is Yara okay?"

"Yea, she's fine. I just changed her, and she's about to eat again. Any word on Yaz?"

"Girl, nobody's told my ass anything," I sighed. "Is Alaya there?"

"Yea, she just showed up not too long ago. Wait, she wants to talk to you."

"Alright."

"Hey girl, Milan told me what happened. You heard anything yet?"

"Not shit, girl they pissing me off."

"So, what happened?"

"He just didn't look okay, and he passed out. I was unable to make out the shit he was saying, and he threw up all over the place in the garage. I've never seen him like that. I hope it's not anything too serious."

"Okay, keep me posted, and don't worry, baby girl is in good hands."

"I know, and I appreciate you both, Lay. Thank you."

After hanging up, almost as if on cue, a middle-aged gentleman approached me. Removing his glasses and clearing his throat, I stood to my feet as he extended a hand.

"Mrs. Cosart, I'm Dr. Jenson."

"Nice to meet you, but you can call me Lemy. Is he okay?"

"He's okay, but after running tests, it showed that he's severely dehydrated, and we found traces of morphine in his system. Is there any injury Mr. Cosart might've had in the past few months?"

"Injury?" I frowned. "No, he's literally as healthy as a horse. I don't understand."

"I'm sure it's all a misunderstanding, but he's stable, and we're currently giving him fluids, so he should be feeling much better really soon."

"Wait, he did suffer an injury from playing ball some years ago. I forgot, but it was so damn long ago."

"Well, his vitals were also skyrocketed, so I may say this has a lot to do with stress. I don't know. With injuries, you never really know. You can suffer some pain every now and then. But rest assured, he's okay and soon as we'll be discharging him very soon."

"Thank you, Dr. Jenson."

Chapter Eight

YAZ

Waking from my slumber groggily, the other side of the bed was empty as I stumbled out of bed and into the bathroom. Yanking the hospital band from my wrist and trashing it, I finished my business and flushed, then washed my hands.

Honestly feeling much better than earlier, but not all the way there, I knew I had to take it easy. Everything's practically been a complete whirlwind, and in order to deal, I might have overdone it with the smoking. Deciding it'd be better to cut back on smoking and drinking altogether, it'd be much harder than possible since I turned to pills, weed, and alcohol to cloud my mind.

Entering Yara's nursery, she was sleeping peacefully. The view just warmed my heart. Bending down to press my lips to her forehead, I left her room and traveled downstairs where noises were coming from the kitchen.

Cabinets were being slammed shut as I walked in seeing all my alcohol bottles now empty.

"My baby is up there asleep, why are you making all that damn noise?"

"Where is it?"

"What you talking about?"

"The fuckin' pills, Ya. Don't you think I know what this is? I've been around to know what addiction fuckin' looks like! And to think I was about to leave you here with my baby? What the fuck is wrong with you?'

"Ain't nobody addicted to nothing, so calm yo ass down."

"You drink yourself to sleep on some nights, every day you smoke that shit, and it stinks up our home, and now this doctor tells me you're popping fuckin' morphine."

Caught red-handed, I stood quietly as she shook her head with a sigh. Rolling her eyes, she continued to pour the alcohol down the drain. It pained me to see her so frustrated. Touching her shoulder, she flinched and backed away, unable to look at me.

"Don't lie to me. Have you been using those pills to get high, Yasir?"

"Lem—"

"Don't fuckin' lie to me," she demanded, pushing my forehead with her finger. "How long?"

"Lem, listen to me. You'on understand."

"Are you outta your rabbit ass mind, Yasir? I don't care what it is. You don't do no shit like that! We have a newborn baby here, and I'm stressed the fuck out, but do you think I'm sitting here getting fuckin' high?"

"It ain't that fuckin' easy, a'ight! I bust my ass daily to make a better life for every fuckin' body, and all I want is the respect I deserve. You can't possibly know how that shit feels when it comes from the woman who gave you life, man. So don't sit up here like you some fuckin' saint!"

"You think I use this shit as a crutch when somebody says some fuck shit to piss me off? No! And you wanna know why? It's because I don't give a damn what a bitch or nigga has to say about me. I know what type of woman I am, and I don't have shit to prove to nobody," she fussed. "Fuck her, and whoever else has some shit to say. Don't allow your conniving ass mother to ruin you, Yaz. Whatever is bothering you, baby, we can get through this. Don't let this defeat you. Use that shit to your advantage, nigga."

"It's not that easy, baby."

"And it won't be," she spoke, holding my face. "You're so strong, and you're so good to me, our daughter, and so many more people, baby. I love you with everything in me, but I won't sit around and allow you to ruin yourself with this. I've seen what this shit can do to people, and I don't want that for Yara or me. I need you, she needs you, and you have to beat this. Please, Ya."

§.

"How is she?"

"She calmed down, thank God," Lemy expressed, rolling her eyes. "How does it feel staying away from work for so long?"

"It's different and takes some getting used to, but I could find myself doing this shit on a daily."

"I'm sure you can," she cheesed, straddling me. "I know it may seem like I'm being overly hard on you, but I'm proud of you and just wanna see you do better. I can't have my Superman fuckin' with the likes of that shit."

"I know, and it makes me fall more and more in love with you to know you have my back the way you do. I just deal with a lot of shit I don't like facing."

"Well, that won't be the case anymore because you got me."

Remaining true to her word, she has been on my ass gradually with kicking this terrible habit. Being that I didn't use to my full advantage, I was thankful to be able to do this without any serious bouts of withdrawals.

The only thing I can really attest to was that any simple thing caused irritation, and in a way, my body yearned a shot of alcohol or a simple pull of weed. It was crazy how much you could initially cripple yourself with the likes of these things and without them, you're faced with your true self.

"Can I ask you something really serious?"

"You can ask me whatever you want, baby. What's the problem?"

"I'm sure some of the shit you've gone through would've been enough to end you. I guess I just wanna know how you managed to keep going, even when it felt like you've given your all."

"My mama would always say that I was a different child. Aneema was more emotional and me. Well, I didn't show any. I guess my emotions were fucked up by my birth parents before anyone could do any real damage. I don't know. I guess it's just how I'm wired, but I just keep going because at the end of the day, I'm all I have. Nobody's gonna have my damn back like I got me."

"How though?"

"If I knew I'd gladly tell you. I don't know you just gotta push through the bullshit, Ya. You've spent damn near your entire life making sure your family was happy and well taken care of. It's time for you to think of yourself now. You're a father now, and we're about to become married in January. If this is too much for you, then let me—"

"Nah," I responded, shaking my head. "It's never too much for me."

"So, let me ask you something."

"What?"

"Are you over your ex?"

"Fuck kind of question is that?"

"I'm not joking, nor am I laughing. So, wipe that fuckin' stupid ass smirk off of your face."

"Whoa." I laughed, slightly turned on. "I'm only laughing because you know me, man. Ain't nobody thinking or worried about that broad. That shit was my mama's doing, not me. You have my word."

"What is up with this bitch and why the hell is she still around?"

"I'on know baby. I wish I had the answer to that."

"Well, I don't want her around. Are we clear?"

"Crystal," I spoke, pecking her lips. "Now can I have my woman for the night, please?"

"You can't have me in that way until these six weeks are up, but I got something else in mind," she teased.

"And what might that be?"

Pecking my lips a final time, Lem pulled her hair into a high pony-tail and climbed underneath the sheets. Taking matters into her own hands, she started to kiss the tip of my dick as her tongue swirled around in a sensual-like motion. Removing the sheets from her face and watching her, she soon grabbed my shaft as she kept her eyes on me.

Closing my eyes, the moment was soon ruined by Yara's whimpers erupted from the baby monitor. Groaning aloud, Lem grabbed the monitor and switched to the camera with a sigh of her own.

"I'll be right back. She's probably hungry again."

"What I'm supposed to do with a hard dick, Halima?"

"Relax, I'll be right back."

Chapter Nine

LEMY

One thing about Yaz's family, whenever the time for family events rolled around, they always threw a grand ass celebration. Dara hosted the celebration for Fourth of July at his place this year, and almost their entire family had come out to enjoy the festivities. All relatives in attendance, along with their liter of grands, older adult children, and all of the above, had come to enjoy some barbecue, boiled crawfish, drinks, and an all-around good time.

For New Orleans natives, this was a normal thing and a time for the family to get together after having not seen one another for long periods of time. For Yara and I, this was our first time being around immediate family, and it was a lot to take in since I'm usually always on Yaz's arm or simply playing my role from the house. No matter how much I tried to talk my way out of this, Yaz wouldn't take no for an answer, and everyone just needed to see Yara.

"You nervous?"

"Are *you* nervous?" I repeated to him. "This'll be the first time you're seeing your mom in how long?"

"About a month or two." He shrugged, securely wrapping his arm around my waist. "I ain't tripping. I told you I'm good."

"If it becomes too much for you, we can leave. I told you."

"This a celebration. I assure you ain't no weird shit gonna be taking place."

"I'm telling you now, I'on want no strangers grabbing or touching my baby without my consent." Completely ignoring my statement as he pushed the stroller, I punched his arm as he smacked his lips and started laughing. "Yasir, so you just not gonna say shit?"

"Chill out, dawg, you're reaching."

"You're saying chill and all that, but don't act all surprised when I cut the fuck up. You're the rich ass cousin who's back with a new baby and woman on your arm. I'm just saying."

"Well, if you're feeling outta the loop, we can always head back to the crib," he assured, kissing my jaw. "Come on now. Do you honestly think they gonna be questioning me when they see how good you fuckin' look?"

"Stop," I fussed, stifling a laugh as he gripped my ass. Leave it up to my man to know all the right things to say to calm my ass down. Calming down and preparing myself, we followed the sound of music and entered where everyone was doing their thing.

Spotting Dara at the grill with a group of older men, my eyes lit up as Alaya had made her way over to us.

"Check out this one with this mean ass snapback! Baby where bitch?"

"Why you gotta be so damn loud?" I laughed as we shared a hug.

"All jokes aside, you look good, Lem," she says, turning to Yaz as they shared a hug. "It's gonna be hard keeping to yourself, huh bro?"

"She knows," he joked, pecking my lips. "I'ma go holla at pops real quick, a'ight?"

"Okay, we'll be wherever Alaya is."

Finding a beautiful shaded area, Alaya went straight for her niece, who was in one of her moods. Removing the shade back from her stroller, she was frowned up and started to open her eyes while spitting out her pacifier.

"Why in the hell is she so damn mean?" She questioned. "Hey, Teedie's Dudi! You look so pretty Yara Bean, yes you do."

"She gets that shit from her father."

"How have you been? I know this is the first time you been out in a long ass time."

"I still have my down days every now and then, but I'm okay." I shrugged. "Your mom's such a huge help, thank you for sharing her with me."

"Girl, she finally has that grandbaby she always wanted. Thank you for bussing it open because I'm not ready!"

Motherhood was a rollercoaster, but I wouldn't trade it for anything in this world. I was thankful for the immediate help that I'd received from Yaz, Anadia, Milan, and Alaya. You could easily tell Yara was initially loved by everyone. Even Dara was head over heels for her, and she currently had every single family member wrapped around her little fingers.

"And to believe your brother came to me talking about a damn nanny. Girl, I literally slapped the shit outta him."

"We were raised to an extent. If it weren't for our families being blended, daddy would've most definitely hired us a nanny."

"Well, I don't play that shit with a bitch I don't know watching my kid, sorry not sorry."

"Which is completely understandable."

"Can I ask you something, Lay?"

"Of course, what's up?"

"What happened between Yaz and his ex?"

"Brielle?" She frowned. "Their breakup was pretty bad, but he never really spoke on why. What made you ask?"

"Gen B has been communicating with her and told her how she doesn't believe Yara is his."

"Whoa, that's outta line!"

"Not to mention, Yaz has been talking to her, and they met up some time ago way before Yara was born. He said it was him telling her to chill on keeping in touch with him or some shit. I don't know, girl. No disrespect, but Gen B is really taking shit too damn far, Alaya. Like how much more can I fuckin' take?"

"I've never seen her this adamant on being so hostile towards any woman. Just be careful because she's ruthless, and I don't wanna see you getting caught in some twisted ass crossfire. And besides," Alaya stated, "she's a thing of the past. I've never seen him this invested in someone, not to mention this half a million-dollar engagement ring. I mean sis, come on!"

Preaching to the choir, I had to agree because she was spitting nothing but actual facts. I'd spent so long being unappreciative with so much because I felt as if I didn't deserve so many things with now being placed in this whole new lifestyle. It felt so surreal. I wanted to be able to enjoy without so many things lingering on my mind, but with everything I've been through, I honestly couldn't help it.

❧

As the party switched into high gear, Yara and I had to take a breather away from the festivities for her nursing time. She loudly wailed while attached to my breasts, soon calming down followed by Yaz demanding to know where we'd disappeared to.

"I'm okay, babe. Dara showed me to one of the guest rooms, so I'm just up here feeding her because she was being a bitch."

"Aye, cut all that out," he stated defensively. "Just bring yo ass back out here when you're done."

"Okay, as soon as she finishes I'll be back down."

Continuing to nurse Yara as I soothed her little curls, she smiled with a mouth full of milk and showcasing her gums now wanting to hold a conversation.

"What are you trying to say, pretty girl? Hmm, what are you trying to tell your mommy?" Cooing and making cute, little noises, I wiped her mouth and fixed my clothing while proceeding to burp her. Within seconds, she released a good burp and couldn't keep her eyes off of me as I kissed her cheeks.

Not knowing a love like this could exist, every single time I looked down at my daughter, I was given a valid reason to keep going no matter how hard it got. Before she was born, I'd always say how I never wanted kids, when, in reality, I was only afraid of doing a terrible job and not having the foundation needed to raise a child. However, this little girl was everything to me, and if I had to endure another painful episode just to assure she was okay, I'd do it all in a heartbeat.

Placing her into her stroller, I heard noises and decided to peek out the door.

Seeing the sight caused my blood to boil. Standing in the flesh with the snake himself, Jhea stood conversing with Indie. Judging by their body language, it didn't take a rocket science to tell that these two were indeed fucking around.

Recognizing that damn voice anywhere, she'd gotten thick and had definitely stayed true to her knack of fashion. Unable to make out what the two were saying, I closed the door and locked it running to Yara's side. Almost as if she could sense danger lurking, she started to whimper which had soon turned to full-blown cries. The doorknob twisted with a knock as I securely held her, trying to shush her.

The knob was being tampered with as it opened, revealing Indie with a mischievous smile on his face. My heart thumped out of my chest, not knowing what this man was capable of, judging by our last encounter.

I didn't know what had me more frightened, the fact that he'd linked up and was now fucking with my enemy or the fact that Yaz was nowhere in sight, yet here I was unprotected with our daughter in my arms.

"Put the fuckin' baby down," he demanded, closing the door and locking it.

"I swear to God I'll fuckin' scream if you—" Revealing the gun in his waistband, I rocked her and held her tight as it sounded while he pointed it at her.

"Let's not put that bastard ass baby at risk now, sweetheart. Come on now. Just follow the rules."

"Indie, I'm begging you...please don't hurt my baby. Please."

"Put her down!" His voice caused her to wail aloud as I shook my head no. Placing the gun at my side, I'd froze knowing that he probably wasn't in his right mind. Shaking with fear, I carefully put her into her stroller as she continued to cry.

"What do you want?"

"You think you can just get the fuck away with all the shit you've done, huh?" Forcefully running his hands all over my breasts and groping my ass, I wanted to throw up because I'd felt so disgusted.

"One thing about your friend Jhea is she'll never know how to work that sweet pussy like you do."

"That was a fuckin' mistake, and you know it!"

"Mistake? Nah baby, we both wanted that shit or did you forget?"

"He's gonna come looking for me. I'll do whatever you want just don't hurt my baby. You know I never fuckin' beg for anything, but don't hurt my baby Indie, please!"

A knocking on the door had startled us both as I froze, hoping it was Yaz as Indie pressed the gun into my side while covering my mouth. Yara's cries grew louder as the door was kicked open, revealing Yaz. In a split second, his curiosity had immediately turned to anger as Indie laughed.

"Come on bro, you know better than to wife a hoe like this. She threw herself at me, man!"

Not even speaking, Yaz tackled Indie to the ground as the gun had managed to fall from his hands. Moving Yara out of the way and screaming for Yaz to stop, he delivered punch after punch to Indie's dome as blood covered his hands.

"Yasir, stop!" I screamed.

Chapter Ten

YAZ

Seeing red and going practically ballistic, we moved all over the guest room. Tuning out Lemy's screams, I wanted this nigga dead. Taking every single punch he'd thrown, I came harder with force knocking him to the ground. Ignoring the pain stinging in my hand, we brawled out like two strangers as opposed to brothers who'd known one another for years.

With my hands wrapped around his throat, watching his life dissipate by the second, I was pulled off of him and snapped out of my trance as I was being held back. Realizing Trevan to be the who'd held me back, I escaped out of his grasp only to be held back by more people.

"Let me fuckin' go, bruh!"

"What the fuck is going on in here?" pops shouted.

"Nigga, I'll fuckin' kill you! You think this shit is a fuckin' a game wit' yo snake ass? I should've listened to my fuckin' woman, dawg!"

"Look at you. This hoe got you all fucked up! Maybe if she weren't so fuckin' loose, then you'd be able to keep her close, my nigga!"

"Yasir," mama fussed, "let's just figure this out, baby. Just calm down!"

"Get yo hands off me!" I shouted, yanking away from her. "Fuck you and fuck him too. How the fuck are you gonna tell me to calm down, and I'm yo fuckin' son? I'm yo blood son, not him!"

"Yasir, son, you need to calm down," Pops insisted. "You don't talk to your mother in that way, not in my damn house!"

"Don't fuckin' touch me!" I screamed, turning to Lem. "Let's go."

"Ya, baby," she cried, shaking her head.

"Are you fuckin' deaf," I shouted, yanking her arm. "I said let's fuckin' go, now!"

Not even caring that I'd caused a scene, I carefully placed Yara into her car seat and slammed the door. I'd thrown the stroller into the trunk and slammed it while climbing into the driver's seat.

"Why didn't you fuckin call me?"

"Baby, he—"

"Don't fuckin' touch me! You fucked that nigga, huh?"

Shaking her head with tears in her eyes, she tried to reach out to touch me, I angrily punched at the steering wheel and tried to contain myself.

"Answer me, I'ma ask you one more time," I demanded. "Did you fuck him?"

Not speaking, she sniffled as my heart broke into pieces. Her silence alone had caused my throat to swell as I'd held back my tears as she once again tried to reach out to me, causing me to look at her in disgust.

Betraying my trust once again and ultimately fucking over everything we'd ever shared, I was at a loss and speechless. Not wanting to hear another word, I sped on home with my mind running.

Arriving home and enduring a silent, filled ride, I grabbed my baby and went to place her into her crib. Proceeding to remove her clothing, I rocked her to sleep. Looking at her innocent face had caused all my current worries to disappear, but I'd known sooner or later, the beast would be unleashed.

Exiting Yara's room and removing my shirt, I stormed into the bedroom to see Lem at her vanity. Enticed strongly by my anger, I'd yanked her up by the arm and stared into her reddened eyes from crying as she screamed.

"Yaz, you're hurting me!"

"You think I give a fuck? I oughta fuckin' kill yo trifling ass!" I shouted, throwing her onto the bed. "Bitch, I'm tired of you fuckin' lying to me when all I've ever done was love yo ass, and this is how you fuckin do me! Huh?"

"Baby, it was a mistake! It meant nothing, and it was before we met, Yasir, I swear to God," she cried. "Baby, please, you have to believe me!"

"Everything I've sacrificed, everything and for you to be lying in my fuckin' face! With the nigga that I called my fuckin' brother, man! Come on, Lem!" I shouted, shaking my head. "Look at how the fuck you do me! And all for what?"

"I'm sorry," she cried. "I'm so sorry for not telling you, Yaz. I just... Please, let's just talk about this!"

"Why the fuck are you crying? I should be the nigga crying! And if you fuckin' touch me again, I'ma beat the fuck outta you! Why man?"

Unable to answer, once again, that unsettling feeling erupted from my core, and I had to step away before I really caused any damage. Turning back around to point at her, my anger had taken over as I wrapped my hands around her throat. She threw punches in an effort to defend herself.

Having a full out fight in our bedroom, she scratched at my throat and pleaded with her eyes as I let go. Falling to the floor and coughing, I'd seen the fear in her eyes and had snapped out of my trance realizing what I'd done.

"Get up and get the fuck outta my house."

"Yaz, no, please."

"Get out! Fuck you and them fuckin' tears. Get the fuck out! You are living in my house and lying to me? How do I even know if you're telling the truth about Yara being mine, huh?"

"Don't do that to me! I'll admit to doing some fucked up shit, but don't you dare bring her into this because she has nothing to do with it!" she screamed. "Yes, I fucked your snake ass best friend years ago, and I'm so sorry I didn't tell you that. Yasir, I'm sorry! But, don't you dare bring my baby into this mess!"

"I want a fuckin' blood test done, and if the shit comes back and she not mine, I'ma do much more than hem yo ass up to the wall. That's a promise. Fuck with me if you want."

"Yasir, w-what are you doing here? And why are you, what happened?"

"Are you gonna keep asking questions or you letting me in?"

Finding my way to the other side of town, Brielle opened her door as I entered. No longer knowing the woman I'd fallen in love with, I was in a shit load of pain that I didn't want to truly feel.

Dressed in her robe and securely tying it up with a face full of concern, she grabbed my hand, and we entered her bathroom, where she began to nurse my wounds. No words were expressed between either of us. Wincing as she placed the cotton ball containing alcohol onto the cut above my eye, she sighed and looked at me.

"What happened?"

"I'on wanna get into all that right now."

"You have a whole woman at home. Just some months ago you told me to leave you alone, and now you're here. What happened?"

"Gimme something to ease my mind," escaped from my lips like a bad song. She grabbed my hand and led me to the bedroom.

Never thinking I'd find myself placed in this position, I wanted nothing but for the pain to end. Time after time, I'd constantly find myself putting my feelings to the side for the sake of others, but now I was just like fuck it all.

Placing the colorful pill onto her tongue as we kissed, she transferred it to my mouth as I swallowed, allowing my hands to roam over her body. She removed her robe, revealing her nude body as she took a pill for herself, crashing her lips to mine once again.

Taking full dominance, allowing the effects of the pill to take its course, she laid onto her back with her legs widened. Removing my shirt and pants, I allowed them to fall to the floor. Kneeling into the bed, she grabbed my semi-erect shaft and began to lick the tip as if her life depended on it.

Fully taking me into her mouth, I didn't know what felt better the fact that we weren't supposed to be doing this or the fact that I was fulfilling my act of revenge. Proceeding to fuck her face, she handled it like a pro and deep throated as her spit coated my shaft. Climaxing without warning, she swallowed and smiled. Without uttering a single word, she turned around on all fours giving me total access as I penetrated deep.

Taking out all my anger on her, her moans filled the room. I grabbed a fistful of her hair as she gripped the sheets. Her arch deepened as the sounds of our skin slapping against one another erupted throughout the bedroom. Falling victim to the pills taking a gradual effect, I thoroughly enjoyed the ride, all of my problems no longer being a worry.

Chapter Eleven

LEMY

"You have to stop torturing yourself, sweetheart," Anadia stated. "We all make mistakes. This isn't on you, Lemy."

"I've never seen him so angry. I don't think we'll be able to come back from this. He hates me."

Just when matters had begun to become too much for me, Anadia had stepped in with her wisdom and kind words. If there were anyone in the world that had known Yaz better than himself, she'd be one of the top names that would come to mind.

Growing tired of holding in so many secrets, I'd told her everything from the very beginning, not leaving out a single detail. Shocked to hear that her dear Yasir had put hands on me, she still didn't judge once I'd told her everything from start to finish. Finally speaking it aloud after holding in so much, she couldn't do a thing except hold me as I cried into her arms.

"Genevie, Dara, and I raised that boy together. I don't care how horrible anything is, he did not have the right to put his hands on you, and I will get on him about it. This crazy thing called love baby will make you do some crazy things. Everything will be okay. It's just going to take some time."

"He doesn't want anything else to do with me. He didn't come home last night. I betrayed him, and this shit is all my fault."

Hearing keys in the door, we both froze as he entered our home. The look in his eyes and the way guilt suited him, I snapped and immediately lunged forward with attacking him. I didn't give not one single fuck, and I followed my intuition, which led me to know that this nigga was out cheating on me.

"Who the fuck was she?" I shouted, being held back by Anadia.

"You'on know what the fuck you talking about."

"You don't come home, and you enter the fuckin' home we share with our daughter smelling like another woman, Yasir, fuck you!" I screamed, tears flowing from my eyes. "I fuckin' hate you!"

"Fuck you, too!" He snapped back. "My life wouldn't be half as fucked up if I hadn't met yo stupid ass! My mama was right, and I should've fuckin' listened to her!"

"Where the fuck was you last night?"

"I'on think that's none of your fuckin' business."

"Yasir," Anadia warned. "Watch it."

"Why the fuck are you protecting her? If you knew what I knew, then you'd feel the same way I do!"

"Yasir!" Anadia yelled. "You were raised better than this, and for you to even come here in this way, I am extremely disappointed. I don't give a damn how upset you are at this woman. You love her, and yes, she made a mistake. Don't you think she knows that?"

"You fuckin' bastard!" I screamed, taking off my ring and pitching it at him. "Was it that bitch? You fucked that bitch and are standing in my face like I won't fuckin' kill you? You're such a fuckin' coward ass mama's boy!"

"I'd rather be a mama's boy, than a conniving ass hoe like you. You hurt me, so I hurt you twice as bad. That shit doesn't feel too good, does it?"

Not even recognizing the man staring back at me, tears once again burned my eyes as my heart literally broke into two. Wanting nothing more to do with this conversation, I removed Anadia's grasp from mine and went upstairs. Heading to my phone, I dialed Milan's number and immediately began to pack some things for Yara and me.

"Hello?"

"Come get me. I refuse to fuckin' stay here any longer with that stupid ass fuck! I'm packing my things now, just hurry."

Thoroughly beat down at this point, nothing could turn back this moment and hearing him say those words to initially hurt me, I knew there was no turning back from this. Though it hurt like hell, I refused to be the bitch that stayed somewhere where she was unwanted.

I don't give a fuck how hard shit may get in a relationship. I'd never turn to an ex for get-back and to know Yaz had fucked this bitch out of spite, I was completely done. I may have kept a secret, thinking it'd somehow protect his feelings, but that was no longer, and before this relationship, I'd rode this thing solo. Nothing mattered at this point except my daughter's wellbeing. He wanted to hurt me, which he'd succeeded in, so ultimately, there was turning back from this.

Milan had arrived as I packed all of the shit I've gotten for myself and my baby. Leaving behind the shit he'd gotten for us, Milan helped as I grabbed Yara who was sleeping. Feeling him staring as I carefully placed her into the car seat, neither one of us said a single word to each other.

Entering the house once again, he was headed upstairs, and once he slammed the bedroom door, I just grabbed the rest of my things, holding my head high.

"Lemy, hear me out, darling," Anadia sighed. "It's gonna take some time, and I know—"

"No," I responded, shaking my head. "He made his bed. Thank you for everything you've done for us, but I can't live like this. I'll call you when we make it."

Nodding sadly, we shared one last hug as we walked hand in hand to Milan's Range Rover.

Pain and change were inevitable. No matter how much you've matured to better yourself from a situation, those growing pains always lingered. I could never fully forget what I've gone through or where

I've come from to get to where I am, but that's just the way life tends to fuck us all.

I had so much to be grateful for, yet these old ass demons refused to allow my ass to be great. Never seeing Yaz and I reaching this point, it had left me with thousands of unanswered questions, and as fucked up as it seemed, space had started to become the only friend I'd needed.

You could forever try to plan a life revolved around a man, but it'd still never go as planned because a nigga will be a nigga at the end of the day. As much as I loved Yasir, I loved myself more, and I was tired of always feeling less of a woman based off of the decisions I'd made in the past.

Days had turned into weeks, weeks a month, and time continued. What seemed to hurt the most had to be the fact that he was missing out on Yara's growing right before our eyes. Struggling gradually with raising this baby girl all on my own, I may have seemed okay on the outside, but deep down, it hurt like hell.

"With both samples given, we'll have the results back in four to five business days. We have all of your contact information, so once these results are given to us, we will be sure to send the letter in the mail. Any questions?"

"Is there a chance these tests could be tainted or tampered with in any way?"

"Nope, all results are confidential and only available to the parties involved."

Using my shades to shield my eyes, Milan and I linked arms while exiting the building. Climbing inside and greeted by Yara's smiling face, I smirked and kissed her cheeks.

"You need to head anywhere else before we head home?"

"No, I'm okay."

Once we arrived at Milan's home, located on the east side of New Orleans, she stayed in a relatively new subdivision. Her home had three bedrooms, two bathrooms, and was very spacious. It was the perfect fit for my friend, and although I felt as if I were cramping her style, she assured her doors were always open for us both.

"Alaya keeps calling me. I don't know what to tell her."

"I'd look stupid remaining cool with this nigga's sister, so I've been keeping my distance. Tell her what you want, I don't care."

"You do care, stop saying that."

"Milan, not today," I begged. "I'm having a somewhat good day. I don't wanna hear anything pertaining to him. Alright?"

"Well I checked the mail, and another envelope was there."

With the orange envelope in her hands, I opened it to see stacks of cash. Weeks after leaving him, these envelopes containing cash had been mysteriously showing up to the house, and although it was unnamed, I knew exactly who it was coming from.

"He's guilty, that's all this is."

"As he should be because he's fucked up for what he did. You only fucked Indie once, and that was to make Hasaan's ass upset. It's not like the shit meant anything."

"He's with Jhea now. The day of the party, I saw her there. I don't care what other shit I got going on, but them linking together can't be good, and I'm willing to protect my baby at all costs with or without the help of Yasir."

"It didn't even make sense for you to do this stupid ass test when you already know who her damn father is. What do you think these two can be doing?"

"I don't fuckin' know."

"You have to tell him. I know you hate him and all of this, but this has to mean something, Lemy. Why else would either of them be together anyway?"

"I don't care, Milan."

"You're only saying that shit because you're hurt, when you damn well know you care. If you didn't, you wouldn't be so worried about him, and you damn sure wouldn't be accepting this money if you still didn't love him."

"If he loved me, he wouldn't have done that shit to hurt me. Milan, I've been through a lot of shit, but it's never hurt this much. He did that to hurt me and with his ex, when I've been nothing but good to him. That's that bullshit, and I don't care, it's not right."

Wiping away the tears I hadn't known escaped, Yara's crying had begun as I looked the time seeing that it was time for her to eat. Dropping the conversation and rushing to her side, not wanting my baby to see me cry, I wiped them away and sniffled.

"Hey pretty girl," I smirked, her hands wrapping around my finger. Her innocent smile kept me going, and although she had no clue what her mommy was going through, she kept me going even when I felt like I couldn't.

Nursing her as she sucked from my breasts, her eyes were a darker shade of brown today. The vibrating of my phone had started. Seeing yet another call from Alaya, I allowed it to ring.

"It's just me and you, baby girl. Mommy loves you so, so much."

Chapter Twelve

YAZ

"You busy?"

"No, you know my door's always open for you." Entering Alaya's home, we migrated to the kitchen where she sighed. "Trevan just left, so it's just you and me, bro. You hungry?"

"Nah, I could use some water though."

"How long has it been since you've gotten some decent sleep, Yaz?"

"I haven't comfortably slept since she left," I stated honestly.

"Well if it makes you feel better, you're not the only one she's ignoring. I've tried her and Milan countless times only to get no reply. You really fucked this up for yourself. What are you gonna do?"

"What the fuck am I supposed to do?"

"Make this shit right."

"Too much damage been done, so that's outta the question."

Having not informed my sister on the damage that's been done on my behalf, she was practically clueless to the real reason we hadn't spoken. Guilt had hit at an all-time high, and without my woman at my side, I didn't know how to deal.

I was a man who had known I'd made a terrible mistake. First, by putting my hands on her and second, using Brielle to fill the void I've experienced from missing Lemy. I was at a loss, and I didn't have a single soul to blame but myself. Not only did I miss her, but I sorely missed Yara as well, and their absence only caused me to spiral even deeper into the dark hole that I was in.

"You don't look so good, and we never keep shit from each other. Besides the fact that you look as if you hadn't slept in days, you look sick. Are you using again?"

"No."

"Anything remotely close?"

Unable to lie to my sister, her look of disapproval was heartbreaking. This was all my fault, and as much as these drugs weren't doing a thing except hurting me, it was the only escape I had to rid myself of these horrid ass thoughts.

"What have you been taking?"

"Brielle's been lacing me with molly."

"I told you to stay the fuck away from that hoe, didn't I? This shit is going to cripple you, Yasir, are you outta your fuckin' mind?"

"What else do I gotta lose, Lay?" I shouted. "Mama doesn't want shit to do with me, my best friend fucked my woman, my daughter may not even really be my fuckin' daughter, and the woman I love doesn't want shit to do with my ass! What else do I fuckin' got?"

"A woman who loves you and a child depending on you! Let me guess. You fucked this bitch too, didn't you?"

Silence consumed me once again as she smacked her lips, shaking her head and rolling her eyes.

"Damn it Yaz, no wonder she's ignoring me! How could you be so damn stupid?"

"She fucked Indie. Did your bestie tell you that?"

"A long ass time ago before she even met you! I may not know what happened between the both of them, but shit happens, and you're dead ass wrong."

"So, you're on her fuckin' side, too?"

"It's not about choosing sides, stupid ass. Right is right and wrong is fuckin' wrong. You're binging again, aren't you? You know what? I'm calling daddy."

"Don't do that, man. Look, I just need to get my shit together alright!"

"Yaz, you're sick! You looked as if you hadn't eaten in days, you battle with depression, and this bitch is feeding your habit knowing that you've had a past with substance abuse! You need fuckin' help!"

No longer wanting to hear what I needed, I'd gotten up and made my way to the door. Exiting and making sure to slam it on my way out, I hopped into my Lamborghini and sped down the streets.

An incoming call on my dash, Brielle's name popping up, I'd answered while coming to a stop light.

"What?"

"I just made it home. You coming over?"

"Nah, not tonight."

"Not tonight?"

"What's wrong? You've been here every night fuckin' me for weeks now, what changed?"

"I can't keep doing this shit with you, Brielle. I'm fucked up to the point where my sister is noticing, and I gotta get my shit together."

"You act like this is your first go-round, Yaz. We've been doing this shit long enough to keep it hidden, but at the end of the day, you're gonna do what you want. My door's always open. If you decide to change your mind, I'm here."

"A'ight."

Never knowing your past could initially come back to haunt you, I was faced with one of the biggest things I'd battled in life. Mama spent years trying to perfect me into believing I was too strong to suffer from the likes of depression. She would often say those genes were silly thoughts and not the problem, so she kept me busy to keep from it.

At sixteen, I started smoking weed in private school. At twenty years old, I was introduced to cocaine, molly, ecstasy, and I'd taken whatever could ease the feeling of loneliness. I'd spiraled out of control and pops caught wind of my abuse, so he sent me to rehab, and once I completed it, Cosart Enterprises was placed into my lap.

I'd stayed sober prior to being CEO of my father's business, and in the beginning, I bid a farewell to my battle with addiction and depression. Upon meeting Brielle, I was thrown into a whirlwind and once again, I'd hit rock bottom. Battling within myself, our relationship was pure toxicity, but we partied hard. It made everything else seem okay when, in reality, we were only hurting ourselves.

I found myself once again at that point in my life, so I broke things off. I took the route to detox on my own. It made me stronger, and before all this stress entered my life, I hadn't thought to turn back the drugs that once brought me so much happiness.

Now, here I am once again, battling within myself and not knowing where to turn with this. Having taken molly or whatever else given to me by Brielle like candy, the only thing on my mind was numbing the pain. It turned into a routine, where some days I'd go, go, go, and not look back.

Refusing to admire myself in the mirror nowadays, I know I'd looked like the walking dead. Alaya knew what addiction had done to me, so hiding this away from my sister was eating me up on the inside. Although Alaya was the youngest, she was very protective, but as much as she wanted to help, this would be a battle I'd have to fight on my own.

Taking it upon myself to travel to Milan's residence, I entered the subdivision as my anxiety began to set in. Having not consumed anything in two days, I knew withdrawals would soon be kicking in, but before that took place, I needed to see Lemy.

Parking in front of the home, I stepped out of my car and made my way to the door, knocking. As I had taken a step back, the door opened, revealing Milan with her arms folded across her chest.

"You have a lot of fuckin' nerve showing up here. Gimme one good reason why I shouldn't beat your ass right now."

"I don't wanna start anything, I just wanna see her."

"Fuck that, she doesn't wanna see you, and no disrespect, but you look like shit."

"Where's she at, Milan?"

A brand new all black Toyota Prius pulled into the driveway. It wasn't too hard to tell that it was fresh off the lot. Emerging from it, Lemy stepped out, and once she caught a glimpse of me, she'd started to get back inside as I ran over to her.

"Stop and just hear me out, Lemy."

"I don't wanna hear shit from you, so get the fuck back!"

Holding my hands in surrender, she stopped altogether and sighed, facing me. Shaking her head back and forth, she shrugged without expressing any words.

"Fuck you, Yasir. I don't care to hear what you have to fuckin' say because it doesn't matter. You ruined us!"

"And it's fuckin' tearing me up? You'on think I know that!"

"Are you fuckin' high?" she questioned, squinting her eyes. "You gotta be kidding me. You're on that shit and come here trying to explain yourself. Nigga, get outta my damn face!"

"I hadn't used in two days, Lem," I admitted. "I know it doesn't make the shit right. I can't function without knowing if you're okay or not."

Fussing a bit and making some noise of her own, Yara was in the back in her car seat. Exiting from the car, Milan met Lemy halfway as she grabbed Yara and traveled inside with her. I hadn't seen her since the fight. We were settling well into August, so I stood stunned at how much she's grown since July, and it broke my heart.

"When's the last time you saw her?" She questioned.

"Lemy, that doesn't matter."

"You're still sleeping with her?"

Silence consumed me as she tried to walk past me.

"Lemy, I need you, a'ight!" I yelled. "I know what I've done doesn't make it okay, and I just wanted you to fuckin' feel how much it pained me to know that you slept with my best friend."

"Yes, I fucked him, but that was way before I fuckin' met your stupid ass. Hasaan was cheating on me with Jhea, also known as the hoe who's been currently fuckin' your so-called snake ass best friend! I wanted to make him jealous, so I got drunk and had unmemorable sex with him Yasir, but at least I'm woman enough to own up to that!" Lemy shouted. "You fucked Brielle to hurt me, and it worked, so go and get fuckin' high with her, and if you know like I do, you better watch your fuckin' back. I'm not the only one they're out to get."

"You could've told me that. Why do you insist on keeping shit from me?"

"Stop it. Don't turn this shit around on me. Even if I hadn't done what I did, you cheated, and you're still fuckin' this hoe! On top of that, you put your fuckin' hands on me. As much as I want to fuckin' kill you right now, I'ma do you a solid and walk the fuck away. Oh, and before I forget," she spoke, turning around and stopping in her tracks. "Thanks for the car, I got it with the cash you've been sending, and the DNA lab called. Your results are in the mail. I'm also getting a lawyer because there's no way in this fuckin' world I'm allowing an addicted, sad excuse like you around my daughter. Stay the fuck away from me, and don't come back here. I mean it."

Chapter Thirteen

LEMY

"Thank you for bringing her. I appreciate it." Dara smiled. "I was starting to think you'd turn your back on us for good."

"No, I just needed some time to piece everything back together."

"He may not show it, but he's hurt. When's the last time you spoke to him?"

"The other day when he showed up at Milan's house. He didn't look so good, and I told him how the results had come in, along with how I didn't want to see him anymore."

"She's going to need her father, Lemy. I know you're hurting, but he's lost. That mother of his did a number on him, and he doesn't quite know how to deal with...how should I say this...drama."

"I've done some messed up things in my life, but I wanted to be a better woman for him. I accepted everything, all of this and all for what? To be called trifling, thrown around, and cheated on."

"Well, you may not know this, but he's battled with depression for the majority of his life and has self-medicated. Gen didn't wanna face the facts that he had a problem, so she kept him busy. Shortly before meeting Brielle, he had gone to rehab. It was terrible."

"I don't wanna be the one to disappoint, but I think he's using again. He showed up looking like he'd lost weight. He seemed so out of it." I sighed, remembering what I'd told him. "Dara, I need to go. Will you be okay with keeping an eye on her?"

"Lemy, what—"

Rushing out of the door and right to my car, I sped to the location of the place I once called home. When you're in a rush to head somewhere, it was almost as if everyone else was taking their sweet ass time.

"Come on, move outta my fuckin' way!" I screamed, slamming on the horn.

Arriving in practically ten minutes, I didn't even turn the car off as I twisted the knob. No longer having my key, I picked up a stone from the fountain and smashed it into the glass while reaching my hand through to enter.

"Yasir!"

My heart was beating ninety to nothing as fear had taken over. Entering the bedroom we once shared, it looked like a pigsty, and as I expected, he'd been binging. The DNA results from the lab laid open on the bed. I rushed into the bathroom where he was slumped over and unresponsive.

Rushing to his side and picking up his head, white residue was underneath his nose. I began to pat his face in an effort to awake him.

"Yaz, can you hear me? Yasir, wake up!" I yelled. "Shit!"

Searching for his pulse, I couldn't find one as I dialed 911 and started to administer CPR breaths and compressions.

"9-1-1, what is your emergency?"

"Please, send help! I think he might've overdosed. He's not breathing. I'm doing CPR right now."

"Ma'am, where are you?"

"It's a private estate. It's my daughter's father, Yasir Cosart. I don't know how much he's taken, but please...just get here!"

"Okay, ma'am, please stay calm. Help is on the way."

Clueless and continuing to perform CPR, I waited for a pulse and had completely tuned out the operator, I prayed and calmed down as tears blurred my vision.

"Come on, Yaz, wake up!"

Hearing sirens in the distance, I continued and refused to give up. With the willpower of possibly saving his life, I started to cry and get a grip because my anxiety was only going to make things worse.

"Ma'am!"

"In the bathroom!"

Stepping away as the paramedics entered, they started to work on him while bringing out the defibrillator. Hoping they'd bring him back, the machine was administered as they immediately placed an oxygen mask onto his face.

"We got a pulse! Let's get him to the closest hospital!"

"Ma'am, will you be riding with us?"

"No, I need to handle something first. I'll get to the hospital as soon as I can."

෧

Thanking Chev for coming through with the address immediately, I looked at the elevator as the numbers dinged signaling that we were at the floor of the penthouse. Arriving at the door, I banged while covering the peephole.

"Who is it?"

Not answering, the sound of locks turning had erupted.

"I said, who is it—"

Decking her right in her jaw, the impact caused her to fall to the floor as she held her face with widened eyes. Shutting the door and turning around, Brielle struggled to stand to her feet as I looked around seeing that her ass was getting high as well.

"You model rich bitches are all the same, huh, fuckin' for the next fix?" I sighed. "You better be lucky I changed my life because bitch you'd be bleeding out on this fuckin' floor if I was the same bitch I was from back in the fuckin' day. I'ma let you in on a warning hoe, stay the fuck away from him, or I will kill you."

"He'll always find his way back," she boasted. "Don't worry. I made sure to keep him satisfied with this pretty pussy he just cannot seem to get enough of. I did you a favor by taking him off your hands. You should be thanking me."

"You better get the fuck outta my face, you crack hoe. Not only did he run to you after I left him, but he had to fuck you while high, bitch. I should be thanking you. Nah, I need to bust you in yo mothafuckin' shit for fuckin' with my nigga, but I'ma let this be a fuckin' warning to you, Brielle...don't fuck with me because I'ma do way more than clock you in yo jaw. Are we clear?"

Speechless, she sucked her teeth and rolled her eyes. Knowing I had her right where I wanted her, I just needed to leave an actual warning. I picked up the blade next to her cocaine on the glass plate and slid it across her face effortlessly.

"You fuckin' crazy ass bitch!"

"Now, this stays between you and me. If I catch a whiff of any police sniffing around me or mine, I'll make sure to kill you and cut you into fuckin' pieces, and then spread the shit all over the city as well as sending your head to your mother for birthing a such a trifling hoe like yourself."

Holding her face as the blood seeped from the fresh wound, I dropped the blade to the floor and politely made my exit.

Arriving to the hospital, Dara, Alaya, Gen B, Anadia, Trevan and Milan were all present as I went to grab Yara while thanking Dara for watching her. From across the room, Alaya approached me with wanting to say so much as she cleared her throat.

"I know we haven't spoken in forever, but I was hoping that we could talk."

"Yea, I see no reason why we shouldn't."

As we left the waiting area for some privacy, the sense of awkwardness was weird being that Alaya and I have grown so close in so little time. In my mind, when you were beefed out with your man, that included his whole family. However, for the Cosart's, that was simply not the case.

"I don't want there to be no bad blood between us. Despite what you and Yaz are going through, you'll always be my girl. You're that sister I always wanted. I may not know the details, but you'll always have a friend in me. I understand your reasons behind it all, and I know you just wanted to protect yourself—"

"Alaya, it's fine. I don't hate you, nor is there any problems with us. I just needed a breather. I was wrong for keeping your niece away from you, and I apologize for that. No matter what you'll always be bound to her by blood, no matter how fuckin' stupid her father maybe, but we're cool. I just felt like y'all would choose sides."

"Never, you can't fuckin' get rid of us that easy," she spoke, cracking a smile. "Is this the cliché part where we hug?"

"I guess so, bitch." We laughed and embraced each other.

Now much older and knowledgeable, at five months, Yara had reluctantly reached for her aunt as we returned to the waiting room where Dr. Jenson was entering just like last time.

"Well for starters, numerous substances, which we would refer to as a drug cocktail, was found in Yasir's system. After looking at his files, it's come to my attention he has battled with substance abuse, which I should've looked at prior to this upon his first visit—"

"First visit?" Gen B repeated. "You mean to tell me this has happened before?"

"Some months ago, he was brought in after passing out. He claimed dehydration, but morphine was found in his system."

"This has to be some sort of damn mistake. My son is no damn addict!"

"Gen, just shut up and listen to the man!" Dara demanded. "Doc, is he okay?"

"When he was brought in, his pulse was very faint. The paramedics spoke greatly of your CPR skills Lemy, and if it weren't for you administering them, things would've turned out much differently. He is stable for now, but I called up one of our finest rehab centers, and an advocate will be here to speak to you all on decisions of having Yasir admitted."

Dramatic as ever, Gen B walked off as I rolled my eyes and kept my mouth closed.

"And if he doesn't agree to go, then what will happen?" I questioned.

"That will be all up for him, but in order to battle this addiction, he will need gradual help. I will also be bringing in a therapist. I'm sorry, but neither of you will be able to see him because he's being placed under suicide hold for twenty-four hours."

"Suicide?" Alaya gasped. "You don't think he did this intentionally, do you?"

"Yasir's primary practitioner has informed me of his troubles with depression, so it's more than likely that this was planned. As I've stated before, rehab is a must, especially for patients in his case. I'll leave you all to it, and once the individual from the rehab arrives, I'll bring him or her to you all."

Chapter Fourteen

YAZ

"You're awake." Pops' voice stemming from the corner of the room caused me to sigh. Completely ignoring it, I felt as I've been hit and run over by a bus. Coughing from my throat being dry, I lifted my wrists where they were tied down to the hospital bed as I gave up knowing that I'd fucked up.

"If you got some shit on your mind man, just lemme know. I've heard way worse."

"How selfish could you be, Yasir? Your mother, Anadia, and I all raised you better than this. What caused you to do such a thing?"

"Well, unfortunately, I'm fucked up, and there's not a thing, you, mama or My Dear can do it about the shit. You'on know how it feels to go through the shit I go through on a daily basis."

"And I don't, but that still doesn't amount up to the fact that this could've ended fuckin' horribly, son. You have this little girl who needs you. Yara depends on you, and Lemy...she's been torn up over this."

"What is today's date?"

"Boy, I'm pouring my damn heart out, and you are asking what the damn date is!"

"Pops, please...just tell me what today's date is."

"September the fifteenth."

Realizing today to be Lemy's birthday, I'd felt guilty as ever being selfish and thinking of my own problems as opposed to her happiness. I was defeated and no longer wanted company, so I asked my father for some time alone.

A nurse entered removing the restraints from my wrists. Something told me to glance up, and I saw Lem entering the room. Looking as if she hadn't slept, I could literally feel the stress stemming from her. No words were expressed as she sat down with a sigh.

Not quite knowing what to say, tears blurred my vision as I turned away, not wanting her to see me in such a vulnerable state. I could go on with saying how sorry I was, but just dwelling on leaving her behind to raise Yara all on her own had me feeling like the stupidest nigga on Earth.

Reaching over and grabbing my face, she wiped away my tears. Her eyes started to water as she wiped them away and held my hands.

"You need help, Ya," she whispered. "Seeing you like that, I didn't know what to do, and if I would've lost you, I wouldn't have been able to live with knowing that I drove you to it. Baby, I don't give a fuck about any of this stupid shit. I just want you to get better. Please, I'm begging you. Don't let this ruin you."

"I'on know where to start," I admitted. "I fucked up so bad, Lem. I never meant to hurt you."

Knowing this birthday would never be the same, on that day, I made a promise to myself, and that was to become a better man. Not for my sake, but for the sake of the women in my life. Ultimately deciding to decline rehab and go through this the harder way, I knew it'd be a long road to recovery, but I was ready to face it.

With disagreeing to the rehab, I'd hired an on-call doctor to keep me on track with clean eating, natural detoxing, and everything else I needed to rid my system of these toxins. Pops held a meeting with some execs, and for the time being, he'd stepped back into his role of being CEO until I was better, which seemed to be the best option.

Lem, despite our problems, had remained at my side every step of the way. The current focus was my betterment, and once I was back to my old self, then we'd start again on building our way up from this mess that's been created. For the time being, she still resided with Milan, and together, we agreed Yara shouldn't be around. Although I missed her sorely, I wanted my baby girl to see her father in good health.

"I'm not eating that shit, man move."

"Dr. Deena says you have to eat or you'll become dehydrated, Ya, you have to work with me. Just a bite."

"Didn't I say no? I'on even know why you in my face begging me to eat when all I'ma do is throw the shit up, dawg!" Withdrawals had ultimately brought out the grouch in me. Although I meant no harm, the lashing out and irritation were a couple of the many symptoms.

Lem was stronger than any other woman I've crossed paths with, and no matter how tough the going may have seemed, she stuck it out.

"Fine, that's you back in the hospital, not me!" Lem snapped, rolling her eyes. "I'm going to check on my baby. I'll be back."

"I thought you were bringing her to see me."

"Not today, Yaz. She can't see you like this. Maybe some other time. I'll stop by sometime tomorrow. I just spoke to Dr. Deena, and she'll be here in a few minutes."

The tension was still on all levels of fucked up, yet she remained at my side through these withdrawals. Seeing Yara was out of the question with the state I was currently in, and it messed with me to the point where I lashed out with no warning.

"You staying with me tonight?"

"I didn't plan on it, but seeing as you're not in the best fuckin' shape, it looks like I don't have a choice, now do I?" Lem snapped. "You need to clean this damn room, and you need a shower."

"If you gonna complain and shit, then you can get the fuck out on'a real."

"Shut the fuck up, nigga. You wouldn't even be in this shit if it weren't for the fucked up shit you did. Don't get mad at my ass because you did this to yourself. You need to wake the fuck up. That's your problem. You're so used to everybody doing shit for you that you get fuckin' pissed off when everything falls on you. You think I'm enjoying this shit?"

"Well if you feel that way, then go! Leave like every fuckin' body who done used me up when it's vital for them!"

"Use you? Nigga, when have I ever used you? All the shit you've done is because you wanted to, not because I needed you because Lemy's been had shit before I met you. Let's get that straight!"

"You see a broad's true colors when a nigga down at his lowest, huh? Fuck you! You're not a damn saint, fuck! You're probably hiding some more shit that I'on even know about!"

"Nah, nigga, fuck you with your sorry ass! You're a fuckin' father and acting like some little ass boy. At least I own up to my wrongs and embrace that shit. You fucked this up, not me! You went out and fucked that bitch knowing how much that shit would hurt me!" she screamed. "Yes, I may not be fuckin' perfect, but I stood at your side, and my stupid ass is still here after you've done me dirty. How can you even say some shit like that to me? So, fuck you, Yaz! Fuck you!"

Nothing hurt more than seeing how much you've damaged a person, solely based on the wrongdoings you've done. My duty as a man is to always protect, provide, and love my family immensely.

Struggling to get out of bed, I slid my feet into my Gucci slides and followed behind her. Arriving at the bottom of the stairs, she hurriedly exited the kitchen and made a beeline for the door.

"Lem," I called.

Stopping in her tracks with her back still turned to me, I made it down to her. Turning her around to me, I noticed the fresh tears streaming down her cheeks. Yanking away, I held her close with all the mustered up strength I somehow found deep down within. She began to hit at my chest. "Stop and just listen to me, baby!"

"Why should I?" she questioned. "Let fuckin' go of me!"

"I'm not ever gonna let you go, baby, I can't," I fussed. "Don't give up on me. Please, I need you. I know I fucked up to the point of no return. I know I hurt you in more ways than one, but don't give up on us and our family, Halima. I can't do this shit without you. Please...I'm begging you."

Emotionally pleading with this woman as she stared into the

depths of my entire soul, I began to get choked up, and although I felt like complete shit, I needed her to know how much I needed her.

As we both stood broken and frightened not knowing what was next for us both, I took matters into my hands with getting on my knees while wrapping my arms around her legs causing her to cry even harder. Partially knowing there was some part of me that knew I'd most likely lost out on the best thing that's ever happened to me along with the symptoms of these withdrawals kicking my ass, I was a literal emotional wreck.

"Please Lem, I can't do this shit without you."

"You've said and done so much to hurt me, intentionally. Ya. I don't know what to do, I don't and I—"

"Tell me you won't give up on me, please...please, Halima. You know me, and you know I'on beg for a single thing from you, but if you left...I don't know what might happen to me, baby. I'm sorry, and maybe this is my karma for taking you for granted and doing what I did, but if it is..., I'll endure it. I'll endure it because I know hurting you was far more painful than any of this shit I'm going through right now. I'm all over the place, and I'm so sorry for being so fucked up, Lem. I wish I were a better man for you."

Still speechless and not quite knowing what to say, she stood and nodded as she bent down while wiping away the tears which managed to escape my eyes.

"I don't know about a lot right now Yaz, but I'm here to fight this with you. Okay?"

Nodding and metaphorically bowing down to her, this was the moment when I realized, even at your lowest, it takes a real woman to uplift and make you better. Resting in her arms, I knew this would be a hard road to recovery, but to know I had her seemed to make the beginning all good for the better.

Chapter Fifteen

LEMY

Pain hit different when the man you always thought so highly of was now at his complete lowest and desperately needed you. In a relationship, the man is supposed to ultimately be able to hold any stress, problems, or whatever is thrown at him, but now, seeing him so terribly torn down physically, mentally, and emotionally, it hurt like hell.

Shivering and sweating as he slumped beside the toilet. Yaz dry heaved and struggled as he attempted to take a sip from his water, only to throw it up. Not quite knowing what to do, I rushed into the bedroom and grabbed my phone to call Dr. Deena, who was on her way but had gotten stuck in traffic.

"Lemy, how is he?" she answered.

"He doesn't look too good. He can't keep anything down, and I don't know what the fuck to do! I'm sorry, but I can't do this." I sighed. "Seeing him like this, I can't—"

"I know. I know, and you can do this, Lemy. You knew it wasn't going to be pretty when you agreed to this, but he needs you more than ever now. I know it, and you do as well. Now, I'm moving as fast as remotely possible. Just keep him hydrated. I may have to instruct you how to administer an IV over the phone if he's as bad as I think it might be."

"Just tell me what I need to do."

With Dr. Deena on speaker, I helped Yaz to the bedroom and placed a bucket beside the bed as he started to mumble something. Fighting with me, I listened while she instructed me step-by-step on how to insert the IV. It was harder than I'd ever imagined due to his case of the shakes. Almost as if God knew how my anxiety had skyrocketed, I was finally able to insert the needle into his vein successfully.

Wiping away the sweat from his forehead as he silently kept his eyes on me, neither one of us uttered a single word. As I looked closely, I noticed the fresh tears streaming down his cheeks. Reaching up to grab his hand, he squeezed and shot up, leaning over to vomit and as my heart ached.

"Dr. Deena's gonna be here, so I'm about to go straighten up."

"No," he croaked, shaking his head. "Don't fuckin' leave me...please."

"I'll be right back. I promise. I'm not going anywhere."

Never in life seeing myself at this point, millions of thoughts ran through my mind as I mopped up our bathroom.

Sometime later, Dr. Deena had arrived, and her timing was perfect because Milan was headed our way with Yara. With being named her godmother, she's been such a tremendous help as well as Alaya, Anadia, and even Dara. This little girl had so much love around her, and as much as things were fucked up as of now, she was the shining light in a dark room.

"Hey, pretty girl," I greeted as she reached for me. "You happy to see mommy, hmm?" Kissing her cheeks as she excitedly smiled, Milan and I settled into the kitchen as I placed Yara into her playpen.

"How is he?"

"Still not in the greatest shape, but he's making it. I didn't think it'd be this tough, not to mention, I'm supposed to seeing Zurich some-time later."

"Your ex-fling Zurich? Bitch, are you outta your mind? Isn't this nigga married or some shit?"

"Yea, but it's not like that. It's strictly business."

To the streets, Zurich Nicola was another well-known name. Pretty much everyone knew of him in the city of New Orleans. Unlike Hasaan, Zurich was more off the radar with his work, and he always kept a low profile. With my niche for being drawn to men of mystery, we crossed paths before I'd even known of who Hasaan was.

Zurich's role was to get rid of any immediate problem that someone wanted to diffuse of. Some would say he was a manipulative killer, but upon getting to know him, I had to learn how I couldn't judge a book by its cover. This man held pain way deeper than anyone I've ever known.

This meeting was specifically to get down to it and rid myself of Indie completely, which would be a tough job being that he's taken over Hasaan's empire. Not knowing whether to watch my back or react on what I know, I called up Zurich. After not speaking in years, he agreed to meet up.

A relationship was out of the question when I'd met Zurich. I was still in school and just getting to know myself. We meshed well, and he was one of the good ones I'd left behind.

"You sure about this?"

"More than sure."

"Okay, well I'm about to head out. Call me later on tonight and lemme know how it goes."

"I will. Thank you for everything, my good sis. I love you."

"I love you, too."

After bidding a farewell to one another, I checked in on Yara, and as expected, baby girl was in her own little world. Traveling upstairs, Dr. Deena was tending to Yaz as I observed from the door.

He looked to be finally sleeping as she emerged from the room, silently closing the door.

"Well for starters, he's slowly gaining his strength back. He's still a bit disoriented, but he's doing better than expected. It takes some determination to wanna battle this thing without the likes of rehab. You really have a strong one on your hands."

"Yea, I just can't take to see him like this, ya know." I shrugged. "So, what's next?"

"He will need to get his appetite back, so that'll be the first thing we tackle, and I'll look for some therapists to assist with him mentally. Did you know of his depression?"

"No, he never even told me."

"Okay, well we'll figure this thing out."

"Um, he hasn't physically seen our daughter. Do you think it'd be good for him to see her now?"

"It depends, how long has it been?"

"Since mid-August."

"It may be good for him, but it's all up to you."

The results from the DNA test proved what I'd already known—Yasir was Yara's biological father. As a mother, I would go great lengths to protect my daughter, and it's partially the main reason why I have been keeping her far away from him as he battles with this recovery.

Looking at her, I saw an even better version of myself, and as much as I hated to admit, pieces of him as well. No matter how angry or upset I was at him, our daughter needed her father, and I wanted that for her since I never really had that paternal figure in my life.

"Can mommy have a kiss, sweet girl, hmm?" Speaking as if she'd known what I was saying, her lips broke out into a smile as she eagerly kicked her legs.

Once Yaz had woke up, Dr. Deena was currently whipping up his daily protein juice as I held Yara while we traveled to the bedroom. Opening the door, the IV had caused him to look a little better, but still not his usual self.

His face lit up immediately as he spotted her. I no longer saw him holding an ounce of pain or sadness. Pure happiness was expressed as she reluctantly went over to him.

"Hey Dudi, daddy's missed you so much baby," he whispered, kissing her as he turned to me. "Thank you for letting me see her, Lem."

"You're welcome, I'ma give y'all some time alone. If you need me, just call me."

Not quite knowing how to feel, I was entering this thing completely blind and anxious for no apparent reason whatsoever. Having not seen Zurich in years, this would be all new to us both since we were now grown, ass adults.

Sitting at the bar sipping on my virgin mojito, I glanced over and there he was. With a skin tone as smooth as dark chocolate, he still looked the same, and not a thing had changed. Standing at an even six feet, his lips broke out into a smile showcasing the gold grill on the bottom row of his pearly white teeth. Those dark brown eyes, which usually held so much pain, seemed to have disappeared and were now replaced with happiness. His then shoulder length locs had cascaded down his back and tattoos covered both of his arms. As I stood, we shared a hug.

"What's good wit' you, maw?" He smiled. "How long it's been?"

"Since Katrina." I laughed. "How you been?"

"Been going through some shit every now and then, but you know me," he stated, sitting beside me.

Still as sexy as I remembered him to be, I glanced down at my engagement ring and back to him as he finished ordering his drink. "You been staying outta trouble, huh badass?"

"Oh wow, lemme not get yo black ass started."

"Come on now. You're already ribbing a nigga when you already know how we do. You sounded real serious over the phone, you straight?"

"I wish I could say that I was, but...you know trouble always seems to find my ass, no matter what. Remember Indie?"

"Snake ass Indie from up on Dumaine?"

"Yea, that's him. Well, let's just say he's on my hit list. Jhea's also outta jail and Hasaan's no longer," I spoke, keeping it short and sweet. "I need him gone, like yesterday."

"You know my policy. I just need that up front, and we gotta deal. Why the sudden change of heart? I vaguely remember—"

"The less you know, the better, Z. No disrespect, but a lot has changed since we've last seen each other."

"I can see," he stated, his eyes motioning to my ring. "Nice to know some nigga lucked up on one of the good ones. He real lucky, I hope he knows."

"I can say the same for you," I shot back. He'd glanced down to the wedding band on his finger and sipped from his drink.

"You're trouble."

"Don't flatter yourself," I commented, standing to my feet. Retrieving the smallest bill from my wallet, I slid it on the counter towards the bartender. "This is for mine and whatever else he's having, keep the change."

"I guess we'll keep in touch?"

"Yea, I'll have that for you soon, and I'll hit you up when I wanna meet again. Okay?"

"Sounds good to me."

"Perfect, have a nice night, Z."

Chapter Sixteen

YAZ

"You look better, how do you feel?"

"I'm not all the way there yet, but it's coming." I nodded. "Dr. Deena mentioned therapy sessions twice a week until I feel mentally equipped, and I'm thinking about it, but now I just wanna focus on me right now."

"And that will happen, son. It just will take some time."

With going through the hardest part of recovery that no one tends to speak on, it is where I'd found myself and knew a change needed to happen. People see my name, then just assume I have it all together when in reality, this is a battle I've dealt with and secretly struggled with for the majority of my life.

Despite every bridge that's been burned whether it being with mama, Indie and confiding sexually with another woman, now I look back and realize I've been spiraling myself into an ever deeper hole I wouldn't be able to dig myself out of.

For once, I needed to focus on my well-being, and for the first time in what felt like forever, I've been doing that, and it felt damn good to freely maneuver without the likes of your family, your business, or the entire world watching your every move.

"Hey, what's up?"

"I was just calling to see where you were, I woke up, and you were gone," Lem stated, sounding worried.

"Pops and I went for a morning walk, and then we stopped to get breakfast. I'm okay. I'll be there in a lil' bit. Where's Dudi at?"

"In one of her moods, but she'll be okay. Well, I was just checking in on you. I'll see you when you make it in."

"A'ight, I'll be there."

"Okay."

Things still weren't remotely back to the way they were between Lem and me, but we both understood some changes needed to be made before we focused on our relationship. Although we still weren't sleeping in the same room, I have noticed the small things and what gave me hope was that she started back wearing her ring, which I'd placed in the room she'd been in some time ago.

"You have a good woman in your corner, she may be a little rough around the edges, but she loves you, son. Don't mess that up."

"Old man, you wanna know what's crazy?"

"What is that?"

"I love her even more than I did before," I admitted. "She's held me down and still is, man. That's more than what I can say for most of the women I've encountered."

"And this wedding?"

"I'on know, pops. I'm just not thinking about that right now. I feel like whenever the time is right, it'll happen."

Arriving home after spending some time to get some fresh air with my father, I made a beeline to the shower. Due to my not physically being able to withstand a full workout, slight morning jogs or walks took the place of that. As of now, all fatty foods and the harsh shit were cut out of my diet, and it was strict clean drinking and eating.

With the help of Dr. Deena, we were able to execute a plan to detox physically while she recommended the help of a therapist to help me mentally and emotionally. I was slowly, but surely getting back to my old self. Although I missed working, I needed this time to start fresh with a whole lot.

Emerging from the shower, Lem was in the bathroom. We stood in awkward silence while I wrapped a towel around my waist. Seeing how she'd gotten flustered, I cracked a smile as she rolled her eyes with a smirk.

"I was just looking for another bottle of my face wash, so don't even."

"I ain't say not a word, where's Dudi at?"

"Asleep, she went back after I fed her."

Moving past her, we somehow managed to get in each other's way, and as she started to open her mouth to speak, she began to look away. Wanting to feel her lips on mine, I pulled her face forward with ease as she reluctantly began to kiss back.

Scooping her up and into my arms, I placed her onto the countertop as my hands rested at her side. Consuming the space between us, she grabbed my hand, placing it between her legs. Her wetness caused sexual frustration as she started to remove my towel while we stopped kissing.

"What?"

"I can't." Seeing the disappointment in her eyes, she pushed me back and hopped down with a sigh. "Lemy, I'm sorry."

"Stop," she pleaded. "Don't even worry about it. It's fine. I—"

"It's not that I don't want to because I do...so fuckin' badly," I stressed, holding her by the waist. "But I'd be a fool to go through with this knowing I'll only be taking advantage of you when I hadn't even proved myself yet. A'ight?"

Calming down, she nodded as we shared one last kiss.

"Just trust me with this."

"Okay, I trust you."

Various scents filled the kitchen as I unboxed the food from its containers, thanking God up above for restaurants. Today had marked two full weeks of my sobriety, and although it was indeed a small step, it was a mark. I was very thankful to have passed with so much support from my family and everyone in my corner just waiting for my progress in the right direction.

"There's no way the both of you are going to eat all of this fuckin' food," Alaya fussed.

"I wish you'd shut up. All I ask is for your help, man. You and Milan always got some shit to say when a nigga is just trying to do right."

With missing Lemy's birthday and honestly just wanting to make things right, I put all things to the side for this specific night. Lemy's done so much along with being by my side. This was my thanks for that.

"Wish daddy luck Dudi and hope your mommy likes this shit because I'm nervous. Be a good girl for Teedie, and I love you."

"She's in good hands, trust me. I'll bring her back by sometime tomorrow afternoon."

"Thank you, sis."

"You're welcome."

Adding the finishing touches, knowing I had a few minutes to spare, I hurriedly went to put on the playlist I'd put together and coincidentally, Musiq Soulchild's "So Beautiful" had begun to play as I turned the volume lower, creating a peaceful and serene atmosphere.

Within minutes, I could hear a car rolling up outside. I looked out the window and saw Milan's Range Rover pulling up. Venturing to the door with a single white rose in my hands, seconds later, the door opened. Everything had taken Lem by complete surprise. She stood speechless as a smile crept onto her face.

"What did you do?"

"You'on like it?"

Ordering a shit ton of both white and red roses, I'd hired a designer to decorate to the point where everything had screamed over the top. Probably overdoing it by just a bit, her reaction was all I'd needed.

"I knew your sneaky ass was up to something! You did all of this?"

"I missed your birthday, and I wanted to do something special for you, that's all."

"Aww, baby thank you. It's so beautiful. You're so damn over the top!"

"Come on and put your shit down so that I can show you the rest."

Taking her hand as she held the rose, we traveled to the kitchen. The music had ended, switching to Avant featuring KeKe Wyatt's "My First Love". She fanned her eyes, speechless yet again as I wiped away her tears.

"Yasir..."

"I know I'm late as fuck, but it's the thought that counts, right?"

Nodding, we shared a kiss as we walked over to the table where I pulled out her chair. The candlelit dinner was the first thing to come to mind with her favorites from her favorite restaurant, Morrow's, an upscale spot featuring the most exceptional dining in the city.

"How's your food?"

"Amazing, thank you. Everything's so perfect, baby. Now I gotta outdo you on your birthday."

"Good luck, but it's not even that." I shrugged, reaching out to grab her hand. "I put you through a lot, and I'm sorry. I never meant for it to go as far as it did. I love you and just having you here with me at my lowest, meant the world to me. I just wanted to show you how much you're appreciated, and I got something for you too. I hope it'll lighten the mood."

"Oh my god, here you go."

Retrieving an envelope from my back pocket, she opened it and started reading. Her frown soon dispersed, followed by a nod of approval.

"Well, it's good to know that you know I wasn't fuckin' you until you got tested. Good job, although I should still fuck you up for playing with me."

"I made a mistake, and I promise to never do that shit to you, but just know I'm all yours from here on out."

"Well, since we're coming clean, I have a confession to make. Let's just say she'll leave you for good."

"Do I even need to ask?"

"No."

"Well, let's do it like this. From here on out, just keep it real with me. That's all I ask and whatever it is, just tell me from the jump. No more secrets."

"No more secrets."

Chapter Seventeen

LEMY

Waking up in my man's arms was exactly how I needed to start my morning. With last night's events replaying themselves in my head, I smiled and turned to watch him sleep. Kissing the corner of his mouth, his eyes fluttered open as he tightened his grip around me. Leaning forward with his eyes still closed, he pecked my lips. I went to his neck and began to straddle him.

"Good morning."

"Good morning, gorgeous," he croaked, his raspy morning voice making itself present.

With his hands resting on my bare ass, I had no idea what had come over me as I stared at him in awe. Morning breath and all, I didn't give a single fuck as we kissed passionately, while we switched positions as he hovered on top of me. With that look in his eyes, completely catching me off guard, his fingers grazed across my stomach and traveled between my thighs.

Inserting a finger, while rubbing at my clitoris, I squirmed underneath his touch and pulled his face to mine. Eagerly yearning for him, he penetrated me as I gasped, moaning out through the discomfort which soon disappeared.

Knowing every spot to his to perfection, his rhythm matched my mind in our meshed symphony. Turning over to my side, he trailed kisses down my back while gripping my thigh and starting again as I gripped the sheets, enduring the pleasure filled ride.

Cupping my breasts, I allowed him to have his way completely with me. My juices flowed so effortlessly creating a well-needed mess. He made love to not only my body but my mind as well.

As the sun danced on the horizon, steadily working its way up into the skies, we still went at it, never getting enough of one another.

Rotating my hips with my hands on the headboard, sweat now coated our bodies as I performed as if we had an entire crowd watching. I breathlessly moaned out as he delivered a slap to my ass while gripping my cheeks and moving me against his shaft. The added on pressure created a bout of euphoria steadily brewing.

As his tongue danced in my mouth, he bit onto my lip as his nails sank into my hips. No words were expressed as he grunted, his orgasm erupting along with as mine as he held me onto his chest. Completely drained, we remained in the same position as he rubbed my lower back and kissed at my neck, gently sucking as I groaned.

"What?"

"Nothing." I laughed. "You just got it outta me."

"I've been missing you."

"I know," I smiled, pecking his lips. "Wanna show me some more?"

"Shit, let's go."

Remaining true to his word, I was put right back to sleep.

Waking up for the second time, I felt around for him only to turn over and see multiple boxes from my favorite labels. Clutching the sheets to my chest, I grabbed the card.

I forgot to show you this last night. I love you. -Y. Cosart

Feeling like a true queen, I proceeded to open the first box from Louis Vuitton, containing the shoes I've been wanting but refused to buy with my money. Thankfully, he'd known my taste to perfection because the Balenciaga shoes and Chanel purses were everything I'd wanted. Though they were material, it meant the world to me that he'd paid attention to the small things.

Showering and getting a late start on my day, I sipped from my coffee while scrolling on my phone. Basking in the comfort of my own home, I wore one of Yaz's old sweatshirts while in my own world. Fighting strongly against calling him to show I'd trusted him, I put my phone down only for it to begin ringing as I answered.

"Hello."

"Yea Lem, I'm here. You forgot about me?"

"Shit Z, I'm sorry," I cussed, sighing. "Gimme a minute, and I'll be there."

❧

I arrived later than the time we'd agreed on. With Zurich's cash in hand for this job to be handled, I pulled up to the location, seeing him posted up against his car. Stepping out, he met me halfway, and I handed him the duffle filled with what I owed him.

"Here's the five racks like you asked," I spoke, removing my shades.

"A'ight, I'm on a time limit or what?"

"The quicker it's done, the better."

Nodding, he opened the duffle as I laughed, causing him to focus his attention on me.

"How long you been knowing me, nigga?"

"You can never be too sure." He shrugged. "So, you mind telling me what the fuck you got against this nigga?"

"He just won't stop fuckin' up my life, so I need him gone. You know I'm private about my personal shit, but I have a daughter now, and I'm willing to do whatever it is to protect her and my family at all costs. Period."

"And your dude doesn't know about this?"

"I'll tell him, but it's not that easy. They're best friends, but it's gotten way too messy, and I really don't give a fuck about it. All I know is that I need him gone. He's untouchable, so I can't get to him like I want."

"And Jhea?"

"I got a personal bone to pick with her. Leave her to me."

With knowing how Jhea rocked, I knew to have Indie removed from the equation was going to do just what I needed. She'll be useless without a nigga in her corner, which is perfect for me to step in.

I was tired of living as if I had to watch my back 25/8, so it ended now.

Returning home and entering the house, I'd heard the television playing in the living room as I removed my shoes and locked the door.

"Hey, baby," I greeted. "What time did you make it back?"

"Just a minute ago," he spoke against my lips. "I was out, so I got Dudi too. Where you went?"

"Out."

"Halima." Only using my name when he was serious or whenever I'd done something wrong, I turned around to face him while grabbing Yara from his arms. Something seemed off, but he refused to speak.

"What's wrong?"

"I just got the call that Indie was killed. Did you do it?"

"No," I replied honestly.

Partially shocked at how quick Zurich had acted, I held my poker face and felt so guilty for not telling him the truth, but he asked a question, and I'd given my honest answer. I may not have caused this nigga's death, but his blood was damn sure on my hands.

"A'ight."

"You need a minute?"

"Yea, I need to call and check on mama. I'll be back down."

The day of Indie's funeral had gradually come around faster than imaginably possible, mainly because Gen B wanted his homecoming services done intimately and just for the family. Not feeling a single ounce of guilt or remorse, I only attended for the sake of Yasir. As much as I was genuinely happy this snake ass nigga was gone for good, I knew I had an even bigger situation to tend to.

"Are you okay?"

Holding Yaz's hand as we left the gravesite, he nodded. He didn't know how to feel, and I could fully understand this because the two were more than friends, they were family. As fucked as it may have seemed, I saw it like this. Indie was better off dead than alive and as much as it bothered Yaz, I did this for us.

A small repast was held at Dara's home, and I hadn't seen a peep of Jhea, which I figured she'd do. Tending to my child and being respectful for the sake of Yaz, I couldn't help but feel Gen B's glares from afar.

Staying true to my word, I refused to give this deranged bitch any time of the day. Yara was much older from being a newborn, but I still was not cool with her being around her, and I made that clear to Yaz. Cool or not, death in the family or whatever, I simply refused.

"You ready to head out, baby?"

Nodding, I stood to my feet as Yara whined and reached for him. Kissing her cheek, she had been fussy all day and managed to calm down once she caught a glimpse of him.

"We about to go, Dudi. Daddy's got you."

"You got some fuckin' never showing up here," Gen B's voice came from behind us, fuming with anger. I looked at her tear stained eyes, not giving a damn as I rolled my eyes.

"And why is that?"

"Nah, it—"

"No Ya, I got this," I interjected. "I'm here to support my man, and instead of mourning like the perfect put together mother that you are for you so-called son's funeral, you're here starting with me. I'm not giving you my energy, not today, Genevie Breaux."

"Did she tell you what she did to Brielle? This is the type of woman you bring around your family, Yasir!"

Not saying a word, he grabbed my hand, and we headed towards the door. Before we could exit, it opened revealing Brielle with the very noticeable scar I'd given plastered across her cheek, and at her side stood Jhea.

Putting it together and noticing how these two had linked arms, it all began to make complete sense. Yaz securely tightened his grip around my hand as we walked right past them. Angry to the point where I was practically fuming on the inside, I held it together and climbed in as Yaz did the same while Chev pulled off.

"What was all that about?" he asked, calmly.

"Me delivering a message."

"I thought you left that shit alone?"

Not wanting to say anything to tick him off, I remained quiet as he took the hint and we endured a silent ride. Once we arrived home, I sent Zurich an iMessage saying we needed to meet up immediately, and he obliged.

Arriving at our regular spot, I don't know whether it was the fact that I was pissed or the way he stood, but he looked good as fuck standing there all nonchalant. Putting out the blunt he was smoking, he'd approached me.

"Are you dissatisfied?"

"No, I'm very satisfied. I just got an even better job for you."

"And what might that be?"

"It's messy."

"When have I ever asked how messy a job was? You know me, maw. What you need me to do?"

"I'm being double-crossed, so I need another one out the picture."

"Okay, and who is that?"

"My mother-in-law."

Chapter Eighteen

YAZ

"I'm hurting her?"

"No, she's just being dramatic. You want me to take over?"

"Nah, I got it. I gotta learn because one day you ain't gonna be here." Struggling with brushing Yara's hair into my poor attempt at a simple puff, she squirmed and fussed with small whimpering.

"Come on, Dudi. Daddy's almost got it, mama."

Lemy's screams erupted from the front door, immediately alerting me as I placed Yara into her swing, rushing to Lemy's side. Hiding her face in my chest as she continued to scream. The putrid smell came from the decomposed head decapitated from a body. She gripped onto my shirt, sobbing as she shook uncontrollably in my arms.

"It's Neema. That's Neema!"

Proceeding to call NOPD, within minutes, our estate was swarmed with the police, a coroner and once again, Detective Paul, who was full of questions.

"Look, man. She was dug up, and her head was decapitated and put at our door! What in the possible fuck type of shit is that?"

"Do you know how long her sister has been deceased?"

"Nah man, it was years ago, and that's all I know. You're sitting up here questioning me when you need to be figuring out who's behind this sick ass shit. I'on mean to be rude and all, but you and yo people need to get the fuck off my property, dawg."

Wrapping his shit up, I immediately went to console Lem. Entering our bedroom, she sat in the dark on the bed with pictures sprawled out. Turning on the light, I noticed a bottle of D'usse in her hands and she was drinking it straight from the bottle.

"You'on need all that. Give it to me."

Wiping her mouth with the back of her hands, she handed the bottle over to me. I joined her in bed as she leaned against my chest while shaking her head with tear stained eyes. Never seeing her so torn up and broken, this behavior was all new to me. Now there have been times where I've seen my woman hurt, but not a pain like this.

Glancing over at a sleeping Yara at the edge of the bed, Lemy's sobs had grown louder as my heart ached because I'd never known the void of having lost someone so dear to you. Even with Indie being dead and gone, as fucked up as it may seem, I felt a weight being lifted off of my shoulders. With our bullshit coming to surface, I guess it just caused me to believe he was already dead in my mind before he physically left this Earth.

"I gotchu always and forever, baby. I gotchu."

※

"Watch your step."

Emerging from the Maybach, Lem grabbed my hand and held Yara securely onto her hip as a small smile crept onto her face giving my hand a light squeeze. Meeting Trevan, Milan, and Alaya at the entrance as Trevan and I shared a hug along with a handshake.

"You ready, big dawg?"

"Always, my nigga."

Newfound happiness had come about, and despite the many troubles threatening to ruin our foundation of love, along with everything we've sacrificed, not a single thing in the world would come between that on this specific day.

"Do you, Yasir, take Halima to be your wife?"

"I do."

"Do you promise to love, honor, cherish and protect her, forsaking all others and holding only unto her?"

"I do," I spoke, my eyes never leaving hers as she cried happy tears.

"Halima, do you take Yasir to be your husband?"

"I do."

"Do you promise to love, honor, cherish, and protect him, forsaking all others and holding only unto him?"

"Yes, I do."

Never fully seeing myself tied down or marrying the woman of my dreams, upon crossing paths with the amazing example of a woman like Lemy, I'd immediately known God her created her just for me. With deciding to make this happen today of all days, I wanted it to strictly be a day we'd both remember and honor dear to our hearts forever.

Classily dressed in a lavender and cream toned mini skirt and jacket set, the gleaming Chanel pin dazzled as the sun peered through the windows of the courthouse. Even in simplicity, Lemy looked her absolute best as I took in every single feature and asset. I couldn't seem to stop smiling at my blessing standing right before me.

This was a forever thing. I was all in, prepared, and ready to spend the remainder of my life with her. Judging by the smile and those happy tears streaming down her cheeks, I could easily tell she felt the same.

"...Yasir and Halima, the two of you have agreed to live together in matrimony and have promised your love for each other by these vows. With the power vested in me and underneath the law in the State of Louisiana, I now pronounce you husband and wife. Congratulations, you may now kiss your bride."

ஃ

Hours later, we soon found ourselves landing in Phuket, Thailand being privately escorted to our villa, only a few minutes outside of the popular location. Wanting to cherish this as a moment being shared with my woman, Yara tagged along. As long as I had breath in my body, my baby girl was going to see the entire world before she'd reached the age of five.

"You think the flight wore her out?" Lem whispered.

"This is light work. She'll get used to it. This is the life of being a Cosart. Y'all better get with the shits." Kissing her hand, she blushed. As she leaned over, pecking my lips, she just continued to stare at me in awe.

"Thank you for everything, baby."

Once settled, I allowed the girls to comfortably rest as I sat outside admiring the island's view. Creating a serene, yet peaceful scenery, the water softly crashed as it rested on the beach. The sun was currently setting, causing the horizon to give off an orange like hue as my phone rang with an incoming call from pops.

"Wassup, ole man?"

"Listen to you sounding like a married ass nigga," he joked. "How'd my girls make out?"

"Both are knocked for the..." Caught by total surprise, Lem stood up behind me. Her hands roamed all over my chest and began to slide down my jeans as her lips kissed at my neck. "Lemme call you back pops."

Hanging up and turning around, Lem stood nude. I closed the screen door and locked it while taking her into my arms. Allowing my phone to fall from my hands, we'd moved over to the couch as she removed the belt from my jeans.

"Where's Dudi at?"

"She's still sleeping. We should be good for a few minutes, so make it quick."

Following Lem's orders, I penetrated the other set of her lips as she winced and started to moan into my ear. Scratching at my back, I slowly moved in and out, then deepened my stroke as she threw her head back in total ecstasy.

Watching my dick dive into her wetness, my thumb rubbed at her clitoris as I grabbed ahold to her thigh and placed it onto my shoulder. Switching the tempo, I continuously rammed myself into Lem as she held on, continually calling out my name. With my lips against hers, the sounds of our love making erupted throughout the room.

She playfully bit down onto my bottom lip, taking my tongue in her mouth. Whimpering and failing at an attempt to move my hand, her legs started to shake immensely. As I held onto her thigh, she pleaded with her eyes, nodding her head yes.

"Ya, baby, you're gonna make me cum," she stressed breathlessly. "Oh, fuck! Ooohhhh fuck!"

Her breasts jiggled on impact as she gave up running away. Wrapping my hand around her throat, she gave a luring smile as her muscles clenched down on my shaft. I drilled in and out of her causing her juices to overflow. Not yet reaching her full climax, she pulled my face down to hers as I deepened myself inside of her a few times more.

Thumping uncontrollably, I let off my seed inside her gut and remained there, allowing her juices to coat me. Her chest heaved up down as I took her onto my lap as she wrapped her arms around my neck while beginning to rotate her hips. Rocking back and forth, then swirling around, I allowed her to do her job as she leaned forward now proceeding to bounce up and down with a perfect arch in her back.

Delivering a well-needed slap to her ass, neither one of us were prepared for another wave of pleasuring which overwhelmed us both. As Lem damn near collapsed on my chest, we remained in the same position in our own mess as she licked her lips. Forcefully bringing her face to mine, igniting a sloppy kiss, I gripped both of her cheeks in my hands and pulled her closer as she sucked onto my neck, licking gently. Climbing off of me, she got down onto her knees and took me fully into her mouth.

"Yaz, baby stop I have to go," I whined, smiling. "Quit it, baby!"

"You're really gonna leave your husband hungry on his first day back at work, girl?"

Never one to be able to tell Yaz no often, I laid back and allowed him to do as he pleased. Bringing back bits of our honeymoon we shared with Yara, I couldn't believe I was experiencing such a natural ass high from this man's love. Everything that involved him had made the details of my fucked up past and life seem so minuscule, which is all I needed to know that I was without a doubt in love with Yasir Dara Cosart.

After being away from work much longer than Yaz planned, he'd be returning with Dara at his side to assure everything ran smoothly. With having grown used to him being home, I was a bit saddened that he'd have to head back, but in the back of my mind, I'd known I could use this time to plot and finally rid these fuckers out of our lives for good.

"Wait, baby. Lemme have a good look at you."

Looking like a full course meal, he had this certain glow about him as I fixed his tie. He licked his lips and started to chuckle.

"What?"

"Nothing, you gonna lemme go or make me late? Which one?"

"Shut the fuck up and come here."

Tasting myself on his lips, he continued to laugh as he pulled away and pecked them once more.

"My Dear will be here in about an hour to get Dudi."

"Yea, I talked to her. You think this is a good idea, baby?"

"She's like another grandma to her baby, come on relax. Plus, she's getting much older and you been with her every day of your life. She'll be in good hands."

"Okay, I love you, my husband." I smiled.

"I love you too, my wife. Make sure you clean this fuckin' house up too."

"Boy, get the fuck outta here!" I laughed, shooing him away.

Once Anadia arrived, I was out the door and headed to meet Zurich. With everything happening so rapidly, I'd told him to put a stop to things since he worked so diligently and efficiently when it came to handling Indie. However, today, things were about to be put back in go-mode.

I've been called every single name in the book, so being labeled a heartless bitch did nothing to me. Once my sister's head was dug up, decapitated from her body, and placed at my door, all bets were off, and I was ready for immediate war. As a hustler, you're groomed to always play it smart. Refusing to fall victim to this sick twisted ass game, I was about to be the bitch to make the first official move that was going to rock the fuck out of this city.

"What it's been about a month, maw?" Zurich greeted.

"Nigga, don't do that. It ain't been that damn long, but I'm sorry I been so AWOL. I've been having a lot of shit going on."

"Change ain't never hurt nobody, no."

"So, I've been thinking, and my mother-in-law is a pain in my ass. I want this shit messy, and I want in on it."

"Lem, you're my girl and all, but I work alone baby. Always have and always will."

"Change ain't never hurt nobody, ain't that what you said?"

"I see what you're doing, but nah maw, I can't do that. I've done some research, and yo nigga is powerful as fuck. If some shit hits the fan, I can't have you around that. It's already bad you got me outing your mother-in-law. Fuck type of shit did she do to you?"

"She crossed me, plain and simple. Have you heard anything about Jhea lately?"

"Nah, she been off the map for a minute. You're handling that, right?"

"Yea, once I get my hands on that bitch, she'll be all mine. But in the meantime, I'ma need you to think on what I said. I'm giving you a week to make a decision, all or nothing, Z."

"Since when did you start giving a nigga orders and shit?" he questioned with a smile.

"Just think about what I said."

Hopping into Yaz's Audi, which I'd taken off his hands for the day as he pushed the Rolls Royce, I changed locations and made my way to Milan's crib. My girl knew all the right shit to say. With not having touched base with her since being back from Thailand, I had to let her know my plans.

"Well if it isn't Mrs. Cosart in the mothafuckin' building!"

"The one and only," I cheesed as she pulled me into a hug. "Damn bitch, if marriage makes you look this good, lemme go find me a scammer!"

"Okay hoe, I'm not about to play with you."

"Where's my Yara?"

"With her Mimi," I spoke, referring to Anadia. "Yaz and I decided she'll be watching her and we'll pay her. Although she's refusing it, we still gotta make sure she right."

"So what's up, girl?"

"Well, I just left from seeing Zurich, and he's refusing to stick to the plan, so I don't know what I'ma do."

"Kill the bitch yourself, plain and simple. We ain't never had a problem with getting rid of no bitch or nigga, and you know that."

"As simple as that may seem, it's not. This is Yaz's mother. If this shit gets messy, he'll never forgive me. I just know it."

"So what you wanna do?"

"First, I need to figure out what these hoes are doing, all three of them. Brielle's a prissy bitch. She doesn't know shit about nothing, but

Gen B and Jhea together, you know they want my head. And that shit they pulled with butchering my sister's fuckin' head is outta line. You know how I am when it comes down to my people."

"Remember Minnie from the nine?"

"What about her?"

"Remember Jhea and her were beefed out for so long? Call the bitch up and have her tell her people that you got a hit out. Knowing her roguish ass, it'll stay out the streets, and the bitch won't know what hit her."

"That sounds good, but then I got Brielle and Gen B. Well, fuck Brielle. She ain't doing too much of shit after I gave her ass a nice slice up. Damn it Milan, am I really about to kill my husband's mama?"

"You gotta do what you gotta do, sis. Fuck how it turns out."

Never in life questioning my work, I was at a crossroads. Not only did I have Yasir to think about, but I knew this would also affect his family.

I know I've changed, but I've never in all of my years of living questioned myself on whether this job was a go or not. Having killed easily within seconds and not shedding a tear or becoming frightened, I was up against this fence on this one.

Awaiting Yaz's arrival home from work, Yara sucked from my breasts as her eyelids began to grow heavier by the second. Removing her and tying up my robe, I rocked her slowly as her chocolate colored eyes remained on me.

"You trying to stay up for daddy, big girl, hmm?"

Cracking a half smile while yawning hugely, she closed her eyes as I held her to my chest. Within minutes, she succumbed into a deep sleep. I laid her onto her side on the couch while surrounding her with pillows.

As I traveled to the kitchen, our front door opened, revealing Yaz with keys in his hands along with my favorite smile. Scooping me up into his arms as he closed the door with his foot, we kissed as if I hadn't seen him in years.

"How was your first day back?"

"It went much better than I imagined, but I couldn't wait to get home to y'all. Where's my baby? Dudi! Daddy—"

"Shh, I just got her to sleep. Damn, you're worse than your father."

"Woman, act like you know," he joked, playfully grabbing my throat with a smile.

Laughing and pushing him away, we traveled to the kitchen. I began to warm up his dinner while he removed his blazer and sat at the table. Just as he began to get comfortable, Yara started waking up. He rushed to her side while I rolled my eyes.

"Daddy's baby knew when daddy got home, huh?"

"You worked on my damn nerves enough."

"Yea, yea whatever."

"Boy, fuck you."

Chapter Twenty

YAZ

"Sir, Mrs. Cosart is on line one awaiting your call."

"Thank you, Becca. I appreciate that."

"You're welcome," she spoke, leaving me to my privacy.

"What's up, gorgeous?"

"Damn, you sound so fuckin' good. If you didn't wake me with dick this morning, I sure would have been making my way to your office quick and in a hurry. It's only been a few days since you've been out of town, and I miss having you around already," Lem purred, sounding irresistible.

"That's because poppa's got that ass spoiled fuckin' rotten. What are you getting into today?"

"I'm having brunch with the girls, nothing too exciting. What about you, Mr. Cosart?"

"A bunch of paperwork, and then I'm headed home to y'all if pops don't need me to do nothing extra for him."

"I'ma have to call my dear, good father-in-law and check-in. It's been a minute, but I just wanna let you know I'm proud of you, baby. With everything you've overcome, and to be back like the shit didn't happen, I commend you. For real Ya, just don't fuck this shit up, or I'ma fuck you up."

"I got you to thank for that, honestly. Trust me, I'on want none of your problems no time soon. We got a good thing going right now, and I wanna keep it up...Mrs. Cosart."

"Say it again."

"Chill out before you make me fly my ass home."

"How you'on know if that's what I want?" She teased.

"Bae, I gotta go. My pops just walked in. I love you, and I'll see you at home."

"Okay, I love you, too."

"Oh no, don't stop on my account." Pops smiles. "Are you settling in okay?"

"You act like this my first day back. Man, I have worked under you before, yea. You do know that, right?"

"I'm just doing what a damn father is supposed to do. Sooner or later, you'll see once Yara is old enough to talk and tell you what she wants and shit like that. Fatherhood is amazing, Yasir. How do you think this whole substance abuse thing has changed you?"

"I'm more open to a whole lot. My perspective is clearer, and I'm more focused than I ever been, man. I spent so much time running away from the realities of my problems. I'm getting there, but I'm in a good space, honestly."

"Are you thinking of seeing a therapist?"

"If things get outta hand, yea, but as far as right now, nah. With the wedding, coming back to work and being stress-free, it's just enough to keep me sane. I hadn't thought about touching a blunt, taking a shot or a pill in weeks. And honestly," I laughed, shrugging. "Withdrawals kicked my ass hard enough to make me not even wanna look at the shit."

"Do you think this distance between you and your mother played a lot in your using?"

"Most def. Mama always was in my corner, but just to see her not fully rocking with my wife and speaking on our child is just outta line. I said it countless times, gave countless warnings, and she kept on. I love my mama with everything in me, bruh, but I'm all Lem has. What kinda man would I be to just allow my mother to continue to disrespect her?"

"Well, I haven't been in your shoes, son, but your mother's always looking out for your best interest. I've seen how happy Lemy makes you, along with how much joy she's brought to your life. It's a joy to see and witness. However, you have to think. It's always been you and your mother, Yasir. I guess she just feels as if she's lost you."

"That's the thing I never even left!" I stressed. "After that shit popped off with Indie, I expected her to be on my side, yet she was protecting him. He wasn't even my blood, and she was protecting this nigga after the shit he did to Lemy."

"All I wanna know is would there ever be any reconciliation on your part?"

"The door's always open. It'll never close, but I don't have time for the unwanted drama shit. Lemy and I are married now. She's my family too. If mama wants to see some change, she'll have to accept my wife for the way she is."

Pops has always been the peacemaker, which is most likely where I get my protectiveness and leadership skills. We meshed well as father and son, plus I felt as if he understood me better than mama.

Falling off with using, hitting rock bottom, and possibly losing everything caused me to realize that I finally needed to start living for me. It was tiring putting myself dead last when it came down to mama, Alaya, and pops. All that changed once Lemy entered my life.

৻৶

Stepping out for some alone time, I made a stop in the Lower Ninth Ward for Gene's Po-Boys for lunch. While stepping out with my food in tow, someone cleared their throat and just as I was entering the car. Chev cleared his throat, and I gave him the nod that it was okay.

The very noticeable scar slanted across Brielle's face was as clear as day to see. Not exactly knowing what to say to her, I waited for her to speak first as she sighed.

"What you want? I don't have the time for this nor do I wanna be seen out in public with you knowing the past we have."

"You blocked my number. I've been trying to reach you."

"For what reason?"

"To sincerely apologize. I know it sounds like bullshit, but...I'm really sorry, Yaz. Yes, we have a past, and I knew your weakness and used it to hurt your relationship because I miss you. However, that ends now, and I can't take it anymore. I know you may not believe it, but I never wanted to hurt you or your girlfriend..."

"Wife, actually."

"I'm sorry, I didn't know, um congratulations."

"Thank you, but with all due respect B, it's not a good look me out here talking to you out in the open like this after the shit we've done. I'm sorry, but I gotta go."

"Yaz, wait. There's something I need to tell you, and it's about Gen B."

"You too, I guess mama a crowd favorite huh?"

"This is serious, look I get your wife and I may have our personal beef, but Gen B is ruthless. This whole thing between you and me was all her. She knew our history, and she knew everything Yaz, I'm telling you...if you care for this woman like I know you do, then you'll keep Gen B away from her."

❧

As I observed Yara sleeping peacefully on my chest, I began to delve in deep thought thinking on how becoming a parent ultimately changes you for the better. Every day I woke up, I wanted to be a better man for my baby girl because she'll always need me. I refuse to have the curse of being fatherless like her mother had placed upon her. As her father, I vowed to protect at all costs.

"You finally got her to sleep, huh?"

"She fought with me, but I got her right. Did y'all have a good day today?"

"Yea, it was nice, but I'm happier to be home under my man."

Still deep in thought on the conversation I'd held with Brielle earlier today, my mind was running rampant. Part of me didn't want to believe my mother was the reason for everything. I had no idea she'd known of my past with using, but you can't honestly put shit past Genevie Breaux.

"Yasir?" With concern in her eyes, Lemy sat up from the other side of my chest. "Are you even listening to me?"

"Yea, baby, I am."

"Oh really?" she questioned, folding her arms across her chest. "What'd I say?"

Before I could even speak, she punched me in my arm as I laughed, smacking my lips.

"Fuck you hitting me for, man?"

"Because your dog ass is ignoring me! Damn, do I gotta suck your dick for attention around this bitch?"

"Whoa, come on now," I frowned, confused. "Calm down, what's all this? You need to chill out before you wake up my baby."

"Fuck you Ya!" she snapped, climbing out of bed.

"Halima."

Slamming the door, I smacked my lips, and sure enough, Yara popped up, crying. After spending minutes finally getting her to calm down, I placed her into her crib and turned on the baby monitor.

Returning to our bedroom, Lemy was in bed with her back turned. Climbing in bed behind her in the spooning position, I kissed her bare shoulder and pulled her closer to me. She relaxed in my arms. As I moved to her neck, kissing her tattoos, she just laid there.

"Are you gonna tell me what's going on with you?"

"Nothing's wrong."

"Stop lying to me, before I force it outta you," I demanded. Turning over in my arms, her dark brown eyes stared into mine as she started to sigh. "Talk to me. I won't know what's wrong until you tell me what's bothering you."

"I just don't want it to seem like I losing you, Ya."

"I'm not going no fuckin' where bae. What are you talking about?"

"I'm just saying, anything could happen and I just... I just don't wanna see anything happen to you or us. Seeing you like that it fucked with me, and I don't wanna see that shit ever again, Ya. Baby, I almost lost you, and I need you to promise me, no matter what, you'll never leave me. I can't do this without you."

Not exactly knowing where this was coming from, she seemed adamant on the issue, so I nodded. Sharing a kiss, she laid on my chest as I held her close. Kissing her forehead, it was then where I realized this was it. I had all I practically ever needed right here in my arms. Even in such comfort, I couldn't stop my mind from thinking back on the conversation I'd held with Brielle.

Chapter Twenty-One

LEMY

Once midnight struck, I slipped out of bed and once again found myself sneaking out to meet up with Zurich to get his answer for the job I'd given him. While driving, I began to have real mixed feelings about this whole thing, along with whether this is what I really wanted to happen.

The stronger my love for Yaz continued to grow, it was almost as if my drive to continue to be this cold-hearted killer was slowly disappearing. I couldn't believe I was turning into one of those whiny ass bitches who's all about her man, but I honestly wouldn't have it any other way because he's changed my life in more ways than one.

Meeting in a much different location, just in case someone Yaz had hired was following me, Zurich was seated in his Range Rover with tinted windows. Parking and exiting the Audi, I joined him inside as smoke from his blunt had filled the vehicle. Rolling the window down as he cut on the air, he licked his lips and waited for me to speak.

"You decided yet?"

"Like I told you maw, I work alone, and it's always been that way. Are you sure this really want you want? This is real muddy, and I've done some fucked up shit to some fucked up people, but this one...I never saw you this adamant on shit like this."

"It's a lot you don't know about me, Z. So much shit has changed."

"I feel you, which is why I need you to really think this shit through, Lemy. This is not just some random ass broad. This is your mother-in-law."

Words from a killer like Zurich had struck something within me. Not only was he speaking facts, but he was also putting it into perspective that just maybe I needed to leave well enough alone. Yaz and I had a damn good thing going on right now. Plus, ever since we've gotten married, all those hating ass bitches have been nothing but a thought.

Breaking my train of thought, my phone began to vibrate with an incoming call from Yaz. Sighing and answering, looking towards Zurich, he nodded as I answered.

"Hello."

"I got up, and you're gone. Where you at?"

"I'm just... riding to clear my head baby, I'm fine. I'll be back in a bit. It's nothing."

"You sure?"

"Yea, I'm headed to you now."

"A'ight, I love you."

"I love you, too."

Hanging up with Yaz, Zurich stared as I playfully rolled my eyes.

"The husband?"

"Yea."

"You'on need to do this Halima, real shit. Just seeing how your whole demeanor changed man, hell nah, if this old ass bitch is causing that much trouble, then she'll get what's coming to her. That's my word."

"Yea, I hear you," I nodded. "And you're right. Thank you for talking me outta doing this, Z."

"Love is rocky, but it's the best thing that's ever happened to me. Even with me still doing what I do, nothing feels better than coming home to my lady after a long, stressful day. Keep your dude close, and whatever problems this monster-in-law is causing, y'all love enough to withstand it."

❧

Returning home at 2:35 a.m. after just driving around the city, I entered the kitchen where Yaz was stuffing his face with leftovers from dinner. Walking over to him and hugging him from behind, we shared a kiss as he pulled my arm to walk over to him while straddling him.

"It's nice to know you're gaining all that sexy weight back, poppa."

"Oh, you got jokes, huh?"

"I'm just lightening the mood."

"You good, huh?"

"Yea, I just couldn't sleep, but I'm good now. It's nothing like a drive around the city to tire a bitch out."

Taking the fork from his hands and helping myself to his food, he just watched as I ate savoring how good it tasted this late at night.

"So the other day at work pops and I was chopping it up. I think I'ma finally go speak to mama."

"Oh, yea?"

"How do you feel about that?"

"Honestly, I'm tired of the fuckin' back and forth," I stated. "Do what makes you feel good baby, I just want my respect is all."

"And you will receive that, even if it's the last thing I gotta do."

Exhausted from today's events stemming from a day out with the girls, dealing with Yara, and handling my wifely duties at home for Yaz, I was literally done for. While cleaning up after putting together tonight's meal, his car had pulled up right on time. Thankfully, Yara had been bathed and was put down an hour prior before his arrival, although she'd probably be waking up really soon.

"Hey baby," I greeted, hearing Yaz enter. With my back turned, the smell of his cologne was all I needed to know that he'd entered, but as soon as I turned around, the glass plate in my hands had fallen to the ground.

Blood was smeared all over his hands and his clothing, and he stood looking disoriented. His eyes were red and low as my heart sank. Wanting to ask so much, I remained on mute as he went to the table.

"W-what happened?"

"Mama's in the hospital. I went to her spot after leaving work, and somebody attacked her."

Like déjà vu, those exact words sounded so familiar, and though this was in no way my fault, the guilt plaguing my ass right now was enough to put my ass on the spot. Joining his side, while helping him out of the ruined shirt, I began to massage his shoulders in an effort to ease the tension when, in reality, millions of thoughts were running through my head.

"I-I'm sorry, baby. Um, is she okay?"

"Yea, she a fighter and—" The ringing of his phone had started with an incoming call. He answered, placing it on speaker. "Yea pops?"

"I'm just checking in on you, son. Where's Lemy?"

Handing the phone to me, I took it and went into the living room for some privacy while taking it off of speaker.

"Hey Dara, it's me."

"Hey, how is he?"

"Shaken up and barely talking. Is she okay?"

"Police are all over it right now, but she was attacked by some unknown person. Her surveillance was knocked out, so we weren't quite able to get a good picture of the intruder. She's pretty banged up and on a lot of pain killers right now, but she's strong, and doctors are giving her a few days to come outta this." He sighed. "I'm here with her now, Anadia and I, but Lemy, continue to keep an eye on Yaz. Neither one of us needs this to have him spiraling again, ya know?"

"Yea, I hear you." I sighed. "Is there anything else you need me to do?"

"Not at all, love, just keep him grounded and busy. I already told him to take the day off tomorrow, but he's refusing. I guess he wants to keep himself busy."

"Okay, well keep me posted on everything. Let me know if anything changes."

"I will, thank you so much, sweetheart."

"You're welcome."

Ending the call and returning to the kitchen, Yaz's appetite was clearly gone. After cleaning up in the kitchen, I'd joined him in our bedroom. Immediately after showering, he climbed into bed and just wrapped his arms around me, remaining in the same position until he'd fallen asleep.

Worried and hoping this wouldn't fuck up his sobriety, I was at a legit crossroads. Waiting a few minutes until he was in a deep sleep, I slipped out of bed. With my phone in hand, I walked outside towards the balcony. Immediately calling Zurich, it'd gone directly to his voicemail, so I left a message.

"Are you fuckin' serious right now, nigga? I fuckin' told you to let the shit go!" I snapped, calming down, realizing he would be clueless as to what I was referring to. "Look, just call me back once you get this."

Calling Milan, luckily she'd answered on the third ring and judging by the sound of her voice, she was most likely sleeping her ass off.

"Milan, are you there?"

"Yea," she groaned. "The fuck going on and why are you calling me at damn near two in the morning?"

"Milan, wake up! I need your undivided attention right now, man."

"I'm up," she fussed. "What's going on?"

"Gen B's in the hospital. She was attacked tonight."

"Okay, which means Z fell through. Shouldn't you be out fuckin' celebrating? Wait, did he kill her? If so, then bitch we popping bottles tomorrow."

"No," I sighed. "That's the thing. I called the shit off, bitch! I told him not to worry about it, so why would he do this?"

"Wait. What? You're not making any sense right now. You did what?"

"I called it off, I told him to keep the cash and..." stopping mid-sentence, noticing Yaz squirming in his sleep, I walked further away while making sure the balcony door was closed.

"I'm here. I don't have enough time, though. Yaz is sleep, and if this shit gets to him, I'm fucked!"

"Damn it Lemy, have you called Z?"

"Yes, but his ass ain't fuckin' answering. What do I do?"

"First thing you need to do is calm down. You know if Yaz thinks anything is off, he's going to flip. Get in touch with Z and get to the bottom of it. This has to be some type of misunderstanding, and don't fuckin' blow this shit because if this nigga flips out, this is on you."

"I know, I fuckin' know. Alright, I'ma go back to bed and try to sleep this shit off. Once Z gets back in touch with me, I'll hit you."

"A'ight, lemme know and Lemy, be careful. Even if this is some type of misunderstanding, keep your shit clean and be aware of certain shit."

"What do you mean?"

"Bitch, just take my word for it, damn!"

"Okay, I will."

Chapter Twenty-Two

YAZ

Tossing and turning all last night had my ass looking like the walking dead, but luckily a hot meal along with my daily dose of coffee would do some good. Checking myself in the full-length mirror, I grabbed my leather messenger bag from the chaise and traveled downstairs. Almost immediately, the aroma of breakfast and coffee had filled my nostrils, causing my stomach to growl.

Entering the kitchen, Lemy stood in her robe with Yara on her hip as Solange's "Stay Flo" played from the soundbar on the island.

"You're in a damn good mood to be cooking all of this, huh lady?" Greeting her with a kiss, Yara reached out for me as I sat at the table.

"I figured you needed a pick me up after last night. You kept getting outta bed, is everything okay?"

"My mind just fucked up, but I'ma be straight. I'ma go see her when I get off, so I'll be home a lil' later than usual."

"Maybe you should just use this day to visit her. With everything going on, I don't want this to overwhelm you. You shouldn't be going to work today."

"Pops put you up to this?"

"We're worried, and yeah, he did. So, what are you gonna do?"

"A'ight I guess I'ma just chill since y'all on a nigga case and shit. Wait, baby, can I ask you for a favor?"

"All depending on what it is, what's up?"

"I wanna bring Dudi to see mama."

As soon as those words escaped my lips, she rolled her eyes with her attitude on full display as she placed her hand on her hip. "Just this once, Lemy. I get y'all got y'all own shit to be worried about, but you gotta ease up."

"You know how I feel about this shit. Regardless of what happened, and I'm so sorry about that, but my statement still stands. She disrespected me, so no I'on think so."

"You're really doing this right now?"

"Yea I am," she stated with an agitated laugh. "You got me fucked up. Enjoy your food."

"You're a piece of work, woman!"

"Yea, yea whatever nigga. I said what the fuck I said, and that's the end of it."

Though we weren't in the best place as of now, she was still my mother, and I was happy to know she'd survived what happened to her.

Last night was supposed to be our sit-down to talk with clearing some things up, but nothing went as planned. Once I arrived at her home, the door was opened resembling a break-in. Alarmed, I barged in seeing her laid out on the floor, barely breathing. She was so fucked up that she thought I was the person who did this to her, but according to doctors, she'd make out just fine. She was bound to be in pain for a few days, and once she started healing properly, she'd be sent home without a problem.

"Knock, knock," the door to my home office opened, revealing pops as he shut the door behind him. "It's funny how on the easiest day, you been cooped in this damn office like you hiding out."

"You always with the jokes, man. You ditched the cane today, huh pimp?"

"Today's one of them good days I will always be bragging about." He smiled, evidently feeling much better. Some years ago, pops was involved in a car accident, which snapped his leg in two. Every now and then he'd suffer pains, which is why he used a cane to keep weight off of it, thankfully, today was one of his good days.

"How she doing?"

"She's awake, but still all over the place. She doesn't remember much of anything, but the nurses got her eating. She'll make it outta whatever this is."

"That shit is fucked me up seeing her like that," I confessed. "I know we ain't been on the best of terms, but I wouldn't wish that on nobody. What is NOPD saying?"

"They're working hard to find the video and decipher as much as they could from it. Once that's done, they'll line up possible people to see if she can line 'em up when she's better."

"I'ma need to call and see if they can get a move on that. This is urgent."

"For now, your mother needs her rest, son, and that's the reality. You're focusing on your sobriety, raising a child, and your marriage. She's in good hands."

"I mentioned possibly bringing Dudi to see her this morning, and Lem flipped out. If it ain't one thing, it's another."

"You can't really blame her, Yaz. Your mother's a tough one to deal with. Plus, you know her and Lemy aren't the fondest of one another."

"Yea, you right. I just thought she'd have a change of mind is all."

"If we were given the instruction manual on how to decipher women, we still wouldn't know it all. You got a good thing going with this young woman, son. She's a special one, don't let that go. I mean it."

"I hear you."

At around four in the afternoon, I'd left the house and had Chev bring me to the hospital. While in route, I'd missed a call from Lemy and called her back, before she started to think otherwise.

"What's up?"

"Where are you?"

"Leaving HQ and about to get some food, why?"

"Come get your daughter. I got a fuckin' headache, and she's driving me up the wall. I don't care where y'all go, just come get her. We just made it back."

"Did you eat?"

"I'm not hungry, I'm just tired, and I can't do that with her screaming after every five minutes, so I'm getting her dressed now. How far are you?"

"Not that far, I'll let you know once I make it."

"Okay, take your time."

❧

"You gotta be a good girl for daddy, Du, and this stays between you and me, okay?" Innocently smiling, I caught her pacifier. We exited the elevator as I pushed her stroller onto the floor where mama was resting.

Going against Lemy's wishes had me feeling somewhat guilty, but she did tell me to take her wherever so here we were. Greeting Nino, mama's newly hired security guard, he gave a respectful nod as I knocked.

Widely smiling as we entered, I went to kiss her cheek and occupy the seat beside her bed, and she started laughing.

"How'd you manage to do this?"

"Ah, don't you worry about all that. How are you feeling beautiful?"

"Like shit," she stated with a faint smile, reaching up to hold my face. "But I'm glad you're here. Your father told me you've been doing good with work lately. How does it feel being back?"

"Once a businessman, always a businessman. Girl, this ain't nothing but slight work."

Making her appearance known by making silly noises, I retrieved Yara from the stroller, and I noticed mama's smile. Blessed with being a happy baby, Yara had known no stranger, and it hurt knowing mama hadn't even formed that bond with her, but this was the right thing to do.

"She's beautiful. I hate I ever doubted her being yours Yazzy because it's apparent." She laughed. "This is all your doing. She looks just like you when you were younger."

"What's in the past is in the past, and we are turning over a new leaf. You're meeting your grandbaby, and I'm sorry I kept you away. Lemy's just protective, and I should've never agreed to such a thing. It was wrong of me."

"Oh no baby, it's okay. I know I can be hard to deal with sometimes, and for that, I sincerely apologize. This isn't my life, it yours and as long as you're happy, then so am I."

Touching base with mama felt all too good, which caused me to miss time like these. Dudi even played her heart out until she'd fallen asleep, and moments like these were all that mattered. They are what kept me whole, and it wasn't until now that I realized I needed my mother just like every man. And after these events which had taken place, I refused to allow anything else to come in between our bond as mother and son.

"Marriage and a baby, I guess I gotta finally come to terms that my baby boy's finally off the market, huh?"

"Yea, she got me, ma. I can't even fight it, to be honest wit'chu."

"I can tell. I just want you to always be careful, and before you start with that attitude, I don't mean any harm by that. You've married her, so you know her better than what I think. I just ask that you be very careful."

"Same goes for you. So this mean, ain't no more beef, huh?"

"Boy, I am not in my early twenties no more. What does that mean?"

"Exactly what I asked."

Waiting for her response, she laughed and nodded.

"Yes Yaz, there's no beef."

Thinking to myself on how well today had gone, I vowed to keep this tidbit of information to myself as I observed Yara sleeping. Mama's words repeated themselves in my head as I sighed, calling Rozman.

"Good evening, sir."

"How are you doing, Roz? I need a favor from you."

"I'm all ears."

"Are you still in touch with that private eye?"

"Yes sir, you need his contact info?"

"Yea, I'ma need that ASAP."

Chapter Twenty-Three
LEMY

Always coming dressed and looking as handsome as ever, Zurich emerged from his Audi sporting all black. His freshly twisted locs were styled into two braids and cascaded down his scalp, while he stood with his hands in the pockets of his True Religion jeans. Black Retro 12's graced his feet. He rocked a simple all black t-shirt and his signature piece of jewelry. A gold encrusted number seventeen hung from his neck, symbolizing his birthplace, the 17th Ward.

"What's good, maw?" Stepping forward as we shared a hug, his cologne lingered in my nostrils as I tried to keep from blushing. This was strictly business, but this nigga was looking good enough to eat.

"Nice to know you finally got back with me. I didn't know you were so busy." Snatching my hands from his, he licked his lips. His vibe was much different than the other times we've met up. He stared at me intently as he shrugged, chuckling.

"I ain't do it. You know how I rock and seems to me she's not just an enemy of yours. I asked around, and she not a stranger to the streets. I heard the old bitch been pushing hella work for years, but settled down once she got wit' yo man's pops."

"Anything else?"

"Nah, not much of anything. You sure she ain't gunning for you?"

"What you mean?"

"No disrespect, but some women just crazy as a bitch. You ain't no stranger to this life, Lemy. Everybody from our walks of life knows this shit is simply what comes with being involved, and when you got an enemy, we all know how to handle it. Maybe this bitch just twisted to believing you a real deal ass threat."

Taking Zurich's words into consideration, I refused to believe this old bitch would stoop as low to thinking I was a threat. Yes, Yaz was my husband, but truthfully, I felt like I couldn't compare to the likes of any nigga's mother because no matter what a man will always love his mom.

"And besides, what type of dude allows his moms to come in between y'alls relationship?"

"A'ight now you're getting too touchy-feely," I warned, smirking and pushing him away. "Does your wife know you touch your ex's like this?"

Wanting to punch myself in the mouth for flirting, I just couldn't help it. With every meeting I'd have with this man, I was always brought back to everything we've been through. Though it was in no way similar to what I've gone through with Yaz, my chapter of life spent with Zurich was practically one worth millions.

"Damn, yo dude finally did that, huh?" Grabbing my hands and admiring my wedding ring, I laughed snatching my hands away from his grasp. I could see a hint of pain in his eyes. "He's a lucky man."

"You must be high or drunk with how nosey you being."

"I just said dude is lucky, that's all."

"As lucky as your wife."

"I'ma go ahead and get on outta here before you get me in some trouble. I'ma keep putting the word out on that info for you too."

"Thank you, Z. That really means a lot to me."

Still holding onto one of my hands and with that look in his beady, dark brown eyes, butterflies formed in my stomach. Images of Yaz and Brielle popped into my mind fueling that anger, imagining the two of them together— my man's dick drilling in and out of her, and my man kissing her the way he was only supposed to be kissing me— lead me to the do unthinkable.

Thinking with my sexually infused mind, I brought my lips to

Zurich's as he aggressively pulled my waist to him. In a haze, not knowing what I was doing was wrong, his hands slid down to my ass, squeezing as he turned me around, so that my back was against his car. Removing my jean jacket and completely forgetting we were out in the open, his lips never left mine as he opened the door to his back seat.

Hiking up my dress as he pushed my panties to the side, his thumb grazed my throbbing clitoris as he inserted two fingers. Licking and sucking onto my neck, I reached down to his semi-erect shaft, vividly picturing how curved he was as he brought his lips back to mine. The memories of how the good times we shared plagued my mind as I froze, realizing how wrong all of this was.

"Zurich."

Reality must've hit him as well as I rolled my eyes, squirming out of his grasp and exiting from the other side of the car. Not even wanting to admit that I'd fucked up, Zurich grabbed my arm as I yanked away from him, shaking my head.

"I cannot do this. This shit is wrong. We're married, and I fucked up tonight. I can't."

"I'm sorry, I had a few drinks and—"

"No, I'm sorry, this is all on me. Fuck! Look, I gotta go. This never happened, okay?"

Not even waiting for him to respond, I grabbed my jean jacket and climbed into the Audi. It roared to life, and I drove, pushing tonight's events to the back of my mind.

&

Emerging from the shower and unable to look at myself in the mirror without the guilt eating me up, I turned away and just stood, recollecting. The average person would call this get-back, especially since Yaz cheated with his ex, but it still was wrong, and I felt like shit for even allowing another man to do what my husband is supposed to be doing.

"You good in there, baby?"

"Yea, I'm okay. I'll be out in a minute!"

Meeting Milan was a must, so I came up with a quick excuse on how Milan was having an emergency with her current dude and with Yaz being so decent-hearted he agreed that I should be at her side.

§

"I've been on edge since seeing your message, bitch what'd you do?" Milan snapped, pulling me into her home.

"I fucked up."

"You're not telling me what I need to know, Lemy. Stop talking in fuckin' circles, damn."

"So, Z and I were talking about the situation, and I'on know what the fuck came over my ass! The next thing you know we kissed and this nigga's fingering me." I sighed, covering my face with my hands. "I shouldn't have met up with him tonight. What the fuck did I do?"

"See, I told you this shit was bad from the jump! Nevertheless, I'm your bitch so I'ma tell it to you straight. At least now you and Yaz are even."

"Nah, not even close to being even!"

"Okay, well then there it is! Why you acting like the nigga dropped some dick off in you or something?"

"Because my horny ass wanted the shit to happen, Lani. Oh my God, Yaz is gonna beat my ass. I can't keep this away from him. You know I can't!"

"If you know what's good for you, then you will. Look, it's fucked up, but he did cheat on you, and he intentionally fucked the bitch. I get you love your husband, but baby he ain't no saint neither. You made a mistake, so the fuck what? You feel bad, so at least you know what you did was wrong. Move on and pretend like the shit didn't happen."

Considering my girl's words, I returned home. Placing my things down onto the island and once again deep in my thoughts, I jumped up feeling a touch and relaxed, only to see Yaz at my side frowning.

"Damn, you okay?"

"I'm just tired Yaz, and please don't walk up on me like that, I almost pissed on myself."

"Come on and let poppa loosen you up."

Shaking my head no, he refused to take no for an answer. He placed me on top of the island, bringing my hands down to his thick shaft while kissing on my neck and sucking gently.

"You really 'bouta turn me down, hmm?" he voiced in a low demanding tone.

He kissed my lips and pulled away at my panties, throwing them to the floor. Pulling me down and bringing my body close to his, he hungrily turned me around as I assumed the position. Teasing at my opening as he held onto my hips, the pressure increased as he penetrated me. Getting his rhythm while pulling up my dress, I pulled it off completely. Delving deeper, still holding onto my hips as I laid on the island, I bit my bottom lip as his thrusts became a bit unbearable, but the pain ached so good.

His dick was hitting the spot it needed to. I attempted to move his hands, but he pushed them away as I whimpered. Opening my mouth to speak, my words were soon cut off by a moan. Turning around to face him, he grabbed my throat. Igniting a sloppy kiss as he slid out of me, I sucked onto his lips and turned around in his arms. Picking me up with one arm and positioning me onto the island once again, I watched as he entered me once again.

Drenching his shaft with every thrust, I felt myself beginning to climax as he sped up. With my breath and words lodged in my throat, I held onto his shoulders as he smiled a bit, deepening his stroke and causing my legs to shake.

"Let that shit go," he demanded. Following his instruction, I allowed my body to release as I tensed up, holding him tighter.

"Fuck," escaped from his lips as he slowed, deepening inside of me, and holding my waist, allowing his seed to shoot into my insides.

Sliding out, I shook my head, no, unable to speak as he chuckled. Hopping down from the island and assuming the position without him asking, he tapped his erection at my soaked folds as he bent down kissing my back, trailing down my spine, slapping my butt, igniting my dripping juices to cascade down my legs.

My mind screamed Zurich who as I threw it back, Yaz quickly matching my rhythm. Climaxing for a second time minutes later, after round two, I damn near fell limp until he'd caught me, and we retired to the couch. Resting on his chest as he pulled a blanket over us, his hands ran through my hair, free of weave, just how he liked it. He kissed my forehead.

Closing my eyes, Yara's whimpers from the baby monitor erupted. I started to get up until he'd stopped me.

"Nah, I got it. Get some rest and I'ma be back."

"You sure?"

"Yea." Placing another kiss on my lips as he pulled on my sweats, he traveled upstairs.

Chapter Twenty-Four

YAZ

"Wait, so who's cooking, Anadia or me?"

"My Dear is cooking with mama this year unless you wanna join. Lay's gonna be there, too."

"So you think you can just drop dick and I follow whatever you say? Wow Ya, I really didn't think you begged me for a bowing down type of bitch."

With the holidays nearing, the first order of business was getting all the women in my life to agree to do one big thing at our crib as opposed to house hopping, but Lemy wasn't having it. For years, it's been a tradition to gather at mama's spot with celebrating the Thanksgiving festivities, but now with Lemy and Yara in the picture, it almost seemed as if things were going to be a little different than it's been before.

"If dropping dick can tame that mouth, then that's what I'ma do. Go and put some clothes on, Trevan is headed this way."

"Speaking of, I need to check on Alaya. I hadn't heard from my girl since she told me was she wasn't feeling too well."

"When?"

"A few days ago, I'ma go see what's up. When's Yara coming back?"

"Uh, I'ma call up pops and see what they up to."

"Okay."

I felt like shit for lying, knowing damn well that I've been secretly allowing mama to see Yara. Today Yara was with pops and mama to spend with her grandparents. With carrying on these secret visits for weeks, and Lem still not suspecting a thing, I knew all hell was bound to break loose once she caught a whiff of what was going on.

Entering my office and checking my computer, my phone began ringing with an incoming call from Roz.

"What's going on, Rozman?"

"Sir, Monty says he just sent info to your email regarding the job."

"Sounds good, let him know I'll have his payment send over immediately. Get him in contact with Jo to get that taken care of."

"Very well, sir."

Although we were in a better place, shit just seemed too good to be true, and the more time I spent mending shit with mama, a small distance between Lemy and I had formed. We make love for hours, she cooks and does all the things she'd needed, but I can't seem to shake this feeling of us not being all the way there fully with each other.

Scanning my e-mail inbox through the countless bullshit, I spotted an e-mail from Monty Jackson. The title read, Jackson Group LLC.

Mr. Cosart,

Attached is the information you asked for. The following dates back to the end of October, up until the sixteenth of November. I sure do hope everything is up to your approvals. Please call if you have any questions.

Sincerely, Monty Jackson, Jackson Group LLC

Clicking onto the attached files, numerous photos popped up and scanning through all of them, one, in particular, had caught my eye. Zooming in and making it larger, there it was as clear as day, Lemy all smiles with the mystery nigga all in her face.

Going through all of them, I'd started to grow angrier by the second. Granted with seeing the holy grail of them all, seeing Lemy once again and this time, her lips were on his, and I started to see red. Powering off my computer, trying to process what I'd seen, I had started to pace and clenched my fist.

Traveling back over to my computer, I printed out the pictures, and I migrated to our bedroom with them in hand. The timing was too perfect as Lemy was emerging from the bathroom with a towel wrapped around her as her smile suddenly faded seeing my face.

"Baby, what—"

"You been lying to me? After all the shit I do for you, you lie and do some hoe ass shit like seeing some other nigga behind my mothafuckin' back!"

"Yaz, you need to calm down, I don't know what you're talking about!"

As I threw the pictures onto the bed, her confusion instantly ceased into guilt.

"I can explain, baby. I swear it's not what it looks like."

"So it doesn't look like you fuckin' around on me, huh? So, I must be fuckin' stupid to you! Either that or I'm blind as a mothafucka because clearly, it looks like you fuckin' that nigga! I'm tripping tho, right? Fuckin' answer me!"

"Calm down," she pleaded. "Please, let's just...Yaz, I swear it was nothing, I—"

"Stop fuckin' lying to me! I'ma ask you only once and I swear to God if you fuckin' lie I'ma fuckin' beat the shit outta you," I spoke in all seriousness. "You fuckin' that nigga?"

At this point, she was hysterical, and tears were streaming down her cheeks. Spazzing out into a full-blown rage, all I remember was throwing her onto the bed as she began to fight back. Completely catching me off guard, she'd delivered a punch to my jaw as I backed away.

Complete fear filled her eyes as she got up, attempting to run as I grabbed her arm, pulling her towards me. Backhanding her, the impact caused her to fall to the floor as she held her face in utter shock.

"You think I'm fuckin' playing wit' you! Get the fuck up!"

"You fuckin' bastard, I didn't even fuck him! So, don't fuckin' accuse me of no shit like that! How could you?" she screamed, standing up and running into me.

Once again brawling like two strangers as opposed to husband and wife, she was getting the upper hand, and I allowed it until she punched me again. Snapping and not realizing the damage I'd done until she laid on the bed, sobbing and clutching her stomach.

"Don't fuckin' touch me! Get away from me!"

"Look at what the fuck you made me do!"

"You said you'd never hit me, Yasir. You said you'd never do what he did to me," she sobbed, shaking her head. "I can't breathe...I...can't breathe." As she struggled to gasp for air, guilt surged through me as I rushed to her side, her body bucking as she continued to struggle, coughing.

Rushing to grab my phone, I immediately called 911.

"9-1-1, what's your emergency?"

"I need a medic. My wife is struggling, and she can't breathe. Send somebody over here right now," I fussed, holding her hand. "Just calm down, help is coming, Lem."

✍

"She has a fractured rib which is caused to believe the shortness of breath. Mr. Cosart, are you aware your wife is pregnant?"

"How far along?"

"It's too early to tell, but once we run the proper tests, we'll be able to get back to the both of you. Has she in any way involved herself in any stressful situations in the past few weeks."

"Nah, not that I know of. She's a feisty one, so who knows but I'll ask to see if I get some answers."

Covering my own tracks although this was entirely all my fault, to say I was guilty would be a complete understatement. My anger has in some ways shocked me, but never did I feel it'd get this bad to the point where I'd fractured my wife's ribs just from one punch to her side. Then, the news of this new pregnancy had my ass feeling like the ultimate fuck up.

Entering her room, her back was turned to me as I approached. Sitting in the vacant chair at her side, she refused to say a word. Tears rolled down her cheeks. She sniffled while I rested my arms on my knees, figuring I'd be the one to break the silence.

"When were you going to tell me you were pregnant, Halima?"

"Good, you should feel like the stupidest nigga out right now."

"Don't turn this shit around on me. You got caught, so you might as well tell me before it gets even more fucked than this situation truly is."

"I don't owe you shit. Fuck you!"

"Nah, I think you do, and you might wanna tell me what the fuck is going on before you piss me off, again."

"You should feel like a piece of shit, beating me while I'm pregnant," she shot back. "What type of man are you? You claim to love me, but just like the other nigga, look at what you do. I cannot fuckin' stand you, so get the fuck outta my fuckin' face before I run my mouth to the highest bidder wanting a story on your fuckin' wanna be perfect, untouchable ass!"

The door opened, revealing mama entering with Yara in her arms as Lemy sat up. Looking at me and blinking a few times, she laughed to herself and turned to Gen B.

"Bitch, I thought I told you to stay the fuck away from my daughter! Yaz, why does she have her?"

"You need to calm down. It ain't even—"

"Why does she have my baby, Yaz? I told you I wasn't cool with this, so why the fuck are you not listening to what I damn well say?" Lemy screams, standing to her feet. "Give her to me! Give her to me now!"

Startled by her screams, mama securely held Yara. As Lemy waited, while standing to her feet, she ripped the I.V. from her arms and pushed me.

"So you gonna stand your stupid ass there and not say shit? You're on her side too?" She yelled, turning to mama. "If you hurt her, I swear to God, bitch I'll kill you my damn self! Yaz, let go of me! Let me go!"

Nurses rushed in, hearing the commotion. As they restrained Lem, she screamed for them to let go. Grabbing Yara and turning her face into my chest, they put a sedative into her arm as she calmed down.

"She's pregnant, man relax!"

"The sedative we've given is not gonna harm her, sir. It'll just calm her down. She'll be fine in a few hours."

Chapter Twenty-Five

LEMY

Mornings weren't typically the same anymore, and ever since being released from the hospital, while asking to take it easy, I've woken up to gifts from Yaz. The haul this morning was gift bags from Fendi, what looked to be ten thousand dollars in cash, and a single white rose. Yaz's presence was once again absent since he has decided to leave much earlier for work ever since I've been home.

Entering the bathroom, beginning my morning routine, my reflection stared back at me. My God, this distress has been doing a number on me. Refusing to give either one of them the upper hand, tears were a visible sign of weakness, which is something I wasn't. A faint bruise still lingered on my side, and thankfully, my lip had healed perfectly. Physically, I was good, but I was broken to pieces deep down underneath this tough exterior.

Entering Yara's bedroom, she was kicking and making cooing noises as her innocent, little face brightened my entire mood. Getting ourselves dressed and officially looking like something, instead of remaining cooped up in the house, I took the Range and drove to Alaya's house.

"Damn, you're much earlier than you said," she greeted. "Aw, you got her looking so cute! Hey Du, mommy's got you looking so pretty, girl!"

Getting comfortable in Alaya's day room, I allowed Yara to crawl at her leisure while we enjoyed brunch Alaya had prepared prior to our arrival.

"You two still not talking much?"

"No, he believes showering my ass with money and gifts is going to make shit better." I sighed, reaching into my purse. "He had this waiting on me once I woke up."

"He's feeling guilty. I mean hell who wouldn't. I just never thought I'd get this bad between you two. He's most likely feeling like shit, but all this can be avoided if you just talked to him."

"I get he's your brother, I really do sis, but us women gotta stick together too. You're always on his side, and I'm tired of it."

"I'm caught in the middle, girl. Cut my ass some slack!"

"Well, you're already automatically on my side since we're both pregnant, so fuck your brother is how I'm feeling right now."

Speak of the devil, my phone vibrated. Already knowing it was Yaz blowing my shit up, I rolled my eyes and answered.

"What?"

"I can't even get a decent greeting when I'm calling to check on you?"

"What do you want, Yasir?"

"I stopped at the crib to take you out for lunch and you not here, where you at?"

"I'm at your sister's house with Yara."

"I'm on my way."

"Nigga, did I say I wanted to go anywhere with you?"

"That sounds like a personal problem. Look, I'm headed to you now."

Ever since our falling out, this man has been adamant on getting me alone, and every single time he's asked, I've turned him down. Alaya claims I was being difficult. Meanwhile, Milan felt as if I were giving his ass a dose of his own medicine. As much as I appreciated my girls for having my back, this was a Lemy and Yaz situation, which simply needed to be handle between us and only us.

I knew it in my heart that it was wrong for a man to put hands on me, but some shit just tends to push a nigga to his breaking point. Not quite knowing what to expect, I purposely brought Yara along with us because I didn't know what type of mood his ass was in. Call it what you want, but I refused to be a punching bag again.

Once he arrived, he took over with putting Yara in the car. Unfortunately, he was pushing the Audi, and this only meant he was going to force me to talk. As we pulled off, I focused my attention out the window. He turned the volume down, and I could feel him staring at me.

"You gonna continue to give me the silent treatment, or are we gonna hash this shit out like adults?"

I've managed to always uphold such a tough exterior mainly because I've been taken advantage of in more ways than one. If we were able to wear our emotions on our sleeve, I'd be naked to this world with insecurities, secrets I've held in and so much other shit that I refused to look back on. I felt as if my trials are what made me into becoming the woman that I am today.

Arriving to one of my favorite spots, Morrow's, the owner and Yaz were familiar with one another, so we were given a private area to enjoy our meal and get to the bottom of things. After getting situated and placing our orders, I didn't know what to say as I observed him playing with Yara. Despite however I felt about him as of now, our baby loved her father, and I didn't want to come between that ever.

"Well I'ma start it off by saying, I never meant to physically cause you any harm," he spoke, clearing his throat. "We've been through some rough shit, but...I snapped. I understand fully why you feel the way you do, but I can't take no more of this."

"You don't care. I'm not your mother or your precious ass business, so I get it. Treat me like shit behind closed doors, and I plaster a smile on my face pretending like shit is okay. You're New Orleans's golden boy, and I'm just the hood bitch who ruined your life, right?"

"Lem—"

"No, you listen to me. I may have fucked up by stupidly making a decision of kissing my fuckin' ex, but Yaz, I've done so much for you, and I've dealt with so much from you, never did I ever think you'd hurt me!" Tearing up, my emotions were on display as I wiped them away, hating myself for crying as I took a breather. "Even now you're carrying on like the shit didn't happen, and it did. When I needed you there, you were with your fuckin' mother, and not only that, you went behind my back with giving her Yara when you know how I feel about her around my child."

"She's still my mother, Lem. I mean yea, we fell out, but what you want me to do?"

"Stop being such a fuckin' mama's boy!" I fussed, shaking my head. "You're saying this and that, but I'm not hearing it. She disrespected me. She filled your head with bullshit about Yara not being yours and now this. How much more of this you expect me to take?"

"What really happened between you and that dude?"

"I kissed him. I don't know what came over me, but I did. We could've had sex, but we didn't. That's the truth."

"You know how fucked up that makes me feel?"

"It doesn't even matter anymore. The damage's already done, and I need some time, Yasir," I admitted, wiping away the falling tears. "I need to—"

"You're not going anywhere, so what are you talking about?"

"I'm not doing this."

"You must've forgotten we married, so whatever problems we got, we sit and work the shit out! Since when have you started running away from shit?"

"You broke me and you don't even know how much that shit hurts coming from you, Yaz!"

"Like I said, whatever problems we got, we sit and work it the fuck out. I'm tired of when shit gets tough, you running away. Last time I checked, you're a grown ass woman and not some lil' ass girl. Yea, I fucked up big time in more ways than one, but this is what you signed up for, and I'll be damned before you just give up on me."

❦

As my eyes fluttered open from a well-needed nap, I observed the surroundings of the bedroom while realizing I was alone in bed. Panicking, mainly because I'd fallen asleep with Yara on Yaz's side of the bed, I hopped out and began searching for my phone which was nowhere in sight.

His switching up had gotten out of hand, and since I practically had no energy whatsoever due to this pregnancy kicking my ass, he's been having a field day with the shits. Typically, I'm upside this nigga's dome with what I want, but almost as if God had a sense of humor, I couldn't do a thing except allow it.

This man is my husband. Even with all the shit we've been through, he'll remain my husband, but coming from a bitch that is so used to making shit happen on her own, this took a while to get used to. My trust was steadily wearing thin. The longer I lasted within this family and upholding the Cosart name came along with some shit neither one of us were quite ready for.

Laid on my side, the door to our bedroom had opened, and within seconds, Yaz was at my side as he sat beside me. Not quite knowing if I wanted to slap him upside his shit or cuddle with him, I kept my mouth closed as he felt my forehead.

"How are you feeling?" Genuinely sounding like the poster boy for good ass husbands, I rolled my eyes, and he smacked his lips. "Come on, I'on need all the attitude."

"Why'd you take my phone, and where's my baby?"

"You needed to rest with no interruptions, so I put it on the dresser. If yo mean ass would've looked, you would've realized that. Du is with my pops. You're in no shape to be running around behind her."

"If I find out she's with Gen B, Yaz I swear on everything I love, it's gonna be some shit."

"A nigga always gotta prove shit to yo ass." Smacking his lips and pulling out his personal phone, he started to dial and place it on speaker.

"Yea, son?" Dara's voice erupted from the speaker as I waited for an explanation.

"Pops, mama near you?"

"Hell no, she's at that house. Why, what's the issue?"

"Lemy doesn't believe that you got Dudi for a few, and she's tripping."

"You tell her Yara's in good hands from here on out." Pops laughs.

"You hear that, mean ass?"

"You still full of shit."

Chapter Twenty-Six

LEMY

"About damn time you're out the damn house. I was starting to think that nigga put a leash on yo ass!"

"Why you always gotta state the obvious shit, bitch? You gonna keep talking or you driving, which one is it gonna be?"

Don't get me wrong, I loved my husband, and no matter how much shit he'd managed to put me through, that nigga was stamped until I said otherwise. This new pregnancy sparked something within me, and I'll be damned before I allow some hating ass bitches to come in between my relationship, which meant it was time to finally hash the shit on out and be done with it for good.

Milan was my ride or die, which meant my bitch was trained to go at any given moment. Finally able to function properly without throwing up and feeling too weak to function, Milan and I were riding out, in dire need of answers. I knew I was fucking around with fire as soon as I agreed to see Zurich again, but this time it was strictly business, and let's be real, I refused to be Yaz's punching bag once again.

"So what'd he tell you?"

"Basically since I'm your fuckin' scapegoat, he's been asking around of this alleged attack on yo monster-in-law. Apparently Gen B's got history with some Piru, and she asked them for a favor."

"See, I knew I wasn't fuckin' crazy. I knew that hoe was playing this shit to the fuckin' tee."

"And that's not all." Milan sighed, glancing over at me. "Look in the glove compartment."

Reaching into the glove compartment, pulling out a manila folder, I opened it and began to scan the documents. I immediately spotted an image of an older man who strongly resembled Yaz. Attached along with his picture was the name, Adonis Carter, who was nicknamed Don and there were many mugshots, dating back to 1970s. My eyes widened seeing Gen B's mugshots and aliases attached as well.

"Genesis Breaux, Viann Breaux," I read, staring at Milan. "What the fuck am I looking at?"

"As I said, the bitch has been down with the gang for some time and still got ties. The nigga Don, she fucked with him heavy for some time, and after going with Z to speak to some old heads, word around town is that Don is Yaz's biological father. The only reason why she was so able to keep it under wraps was because Dara was blinded and was under the impression he had no reason not to believe her. Z did the honors of asking around of Don, but he was killed back in 1992."

"Yaz was born in '92." I sighed. "This shit is gonna crush him. Who knew she was this fuckin' crazy?"

"That's not it, bitch. Guess who she hired to do the job?"

"Who?"

"Jhea."

"That's just like two miserable ass bitches to gang up on a bitch trying to be right, and shit, I'ma be sure to nip this in the bud."

Going against all things, Milan and I pulled up to Zurich's home. According to Milan, his wife wasn't home, and it was a relief because there needed to be no tension between either one of us.

As expected, his home was located in a very suburban area, far out in the east. Ever since the storm, it was almost as if all the real roguish and ghetto parts were occupied by the wealthier folk, mainly the whites. Despite his choice of making a living, this man was honestly intelligent as fuck, and whenever he wasn't fucking off doing horrid shit, he dabbled a bit in stocks and exchange, he basically lived a double life.

Almost as if this baby had known I was somewhere I didn't need to be, I immediately felt the sudden urge to throw up. Taking a few sips of water while pulling it together, Milan and I exited the car, then approached his door.

"You sure you good?"

"I'm forever good. Let's just get this shit over with."

Milan took the initiative to knock, and as soon as she did, the door just pushed open on its own. Off the rip, I got a vibe as she almost walked in until I stopped her.

"Are you outta your mind?!"

"Outta my mind for what? Get your damn hands off and stop acting so fuckin' scary!"

"Milan, you can't just waltz into this nigga's house like this!"

"Watch me, bitch." Completely ignoring my statement and stepping inside as if she owned the place, I began to grow nauseous once again.

"Z!" Milan shouted.

"We need to fuckin' go!"

Stopping in her tracks, a blood trail starting from the living room and into the kitchen had caught our attention. Inching further, I covered my mouth and immediately could no longer hold my vomit as I ran over to the sink, hurling uncontrollably.

"Is he dead?"

"Yes, the nigga is dead! We need to go, Milan. Like now!"

A single bullet wound to the head was what did it, and as I looked at Z's lifeless body, a pool of blood formed around him, I knew we had to get out of here and quick. My eyes had seen it, but I still couldn't fully process that he was gone. Our last encounter had come rushing back to me as I wiped away a stray tear, sniffling, and breaking the silence.

"When was the last time you talked to him?"

"Like two fuckin' nights ago. Damn, who could've done this shit to him?"

Not even answering, she and I looked at one another as she suddenly slammed on breaks as a cream colored Mitsubishi with tinted windows had pulled out recklessly in front of us. It was about four o'clock in the day, and the street was literally vacant as my heart began to thump out of my chest. Milan read my mind, immediately putting her car into reverse, whipping around, and then hitting the gas.

Checking the rearview mirror, the car wasn't too far behind. Gunshots rang out, causing us to duck. My girl always stayed strapped, and once I checked underneath the seat, I found her gun fully loaded, I rolled down the window, aiming for the car. Ducking as more bullets flew from behind us as Milan swerved, causing the gun to fall from my hands and the car to start beeping.

"Shit, they got my back tire!"

"I don't give a fuck, just drive!"

Once I turned around once again, they were long gone and luckily, we were out of the neighborhood, but Milan couldn't drive any further with a flat tire. My nerves were shot to shit as we pulled in the Walgreen's parking lot. I opened the door, throwing up again as Milan scoffed, shaking her head.

"You couldn't hold that shit in?"

"Fuck you and get us the fuck up outta here."

Staring at the time on my iPad, it read *8:03 p.m.* as lights reflected themselves into the bedroom, Yaz's Maybach pulled up into our yard. A sense of relief washed over me as I carefully climbed out of bed, kissing Yara's cheek and rushing downstairs to meet him at the door.

Today's been a long ass day, and I wanted nothing more than to be surrounded by my man. The door opened, and as he entered, I practically ran into his arms before he could even put down the keys. Almost as if on cue, I'd begun crying. He grabbed my face, and I just started to sob uncontrollably. He sighed, pulling me into his chest.

Minutes later, we were resting on the couch as I tried to piece together how I'd tell him everything from start to finish. At this point, there was no keeping anything from him. As much as this would fuck him up, I needed him to know the stakes were much higher than we thought.

"What's got you so fuckin' upset?" Thumbing away my tears, his voice was full of concern as he pressed his lips to my forehead.

As I looked at him, I couldn't bare breaking him down after seeing how he's been at rock bottom, yet still managed to hold it all together. Withholding this information was a terrible thing, but once he knew of everything I was holding in, I somehow knew that after today, he would no longer be my perfect man. This info could literally break him down much worse than addiction has, and I loved him so much that I couldn't fathom being the reason behind his unhappiness.

To protect his heart and most importantly, his mind, I did the unthinkable.

"I'm just having one of those days. I know you get tired of me crying all the time and—"

"No baby, never that. You scared me for a minute," he chuckled, smiling a bit as he caressed my cheek. "I can't have my strong baby getting all sappy on a nigga, no."

"Can we get away for a minute? I don't care where we go. I just need to leave New Orleans. Just you, me and Yara."

"I can't, I—"

"Please Ya, you know I don't beg for shit, but I need to get away. I'm so fuckin' stressed out all the time, and I need to release this. Please?"

"A'ight, I'ma work something out."

Chapter Twenty-Seven

YAZ

Nothing in this world felt more peaceful than being able to willingly pack up and high tail away from all the drama shit, especially when you were with the ones who mattered the most. As the sun began setting on the horizon, creating this orange like hue, goose-bumps formed on my arms as her touch traveled up my arms while her lips pressed against the back of my shoulder.

To a man, not knowing what had your woman all over the place was frustrating. I had known Lemy like the back of my hands, and she was much stronger than any woman I've ever crossed paths with. Seeing her so torn up on that day that I returned from home from work was a lot to take in. Women like her, you can't continue to pry and possibly pull out whatever is bothering her, but you got to have some sense of patience.

Any woman placed in a similar situation would react completely differently, but she was doing the best she possibly could all while pregnant, dealing with my mother's shit from time to time, and not even having a mother of her own to fall back on. As I began putting it all into perspective, I started to realize maybe a life without all this drama was exactly what we needed.

Businesswise pops wanted to expand, and though New Orleans

would always be my home, I felt like a fresh start was needed. December was steadily winding down, and before you know it, Christmas would be here. Yara would be turning a year old in May, we'd also be welcoming this new baby into the family, and as this year neared its end, I couldn't help but continue thinking of possibilities for our future.

Before meeting Lem, I was all about work and didn't do a damn thing except fuck off all while making money. Times were much different, it was no longer about me, but I had a family to provide for and those bachelor, playboy days were over.

"What are you thinking about?"

Breaking my train of thought, she stepped in front me with genuine concern expressed all over her face. Bending down to kiss her lips, reassuring her, I was straight. She smiled, allowing her fingers to trail down my chest.

Before going any further, my phone had started to ring. Lem sighed and started to roll her eyes.

"Fuck that phone."

"I gotta answer it, bae."

Mama's name flashed on the screen as I answered. Lemy gave me some privacy as I sat in the lounge chair.

"Yes, ma'am?"

"I stopped by the house, and everyone's gone, where are you?"

"Lem wanted to get outta town, so we had a lil' getaway for the rest of the week. I'm surprised pops ain't call you."

"That damn father of yours never calls me boy. You know that. You still didn't answer my question either, Yazzy."

"Oh, we in Florida. I buy so many houses that I tend to forget I got 'em in different places."

"Alright then, chile. Kiss my grandbaby for me, and I'll see you when you make it back."

"A'ight."

Entering the master bedroom, Lemy was rocking Yara to sleep, and as soon as I climbed in the bed, she started to fight her sleep. Reaching for her, she jumped into my arms and laid her head against my chest.

"Why can't it always be like this, baby?"

"Wat'chu mean? This shit is not only for me. This is yours too."
Unable to quite read her emotions, she looked at me and turned away.
"What's gotten into you?"

"I have just been thinking about a lot and...I wanna leave New
Orleans. Ya, I got nothing but badass memories, and it's not just us
now, I know you have work, but can't you work something out with
Dara?"

"It's crazy you say that because I been thinking a lot on that, too.
Not only that, but I see how uncomfortable you are now, and it
bothers me. Pops sighed off on expansion, and the first place we're
shooting for is Miami."

"You don't feel like I'm making you chose?"

"This shit is not about just me. I got some demons back at home
just as well as you. Whatever you wanna do, you just gotta lemme
know. If you want to move somewhere, tell me."

"You're so close to your family though, baby. I don't want it to seem
like I'm the reason behind y'all falling apart."

"That'll never be the case. I'm married to you, we got a daughter to
raise and a newborn to welcome into this world in a few months. I'm
wit'chu on whatever. I told you that from the jump. It's you and me
always and forever."

"Okay, I hear you."

Upon returning home, the countdown until Christmas was in total
effect. Along with preparing, Lemy had also got around to attending
her first prenatal appointment where we'd discovered she was almost
ten weeks. Everything, for now, was going perfectly, and I don't know
whether it was the most joyous time of the year that had an effect on
us all or what, but these all out good vibes were much needed.

"I'm not the only pregnant one here, and I'm sorry but watching
you two suck face is making my ass nauseous, so fuckin' stop so that we
can finish wrapping this shit!" Alaya's words went in one ear and out
the other as I stuck up my middle finger, happily kissing my wife the
way I wanted.

"No, wait," she whimpered, pouting as she pulled my face back to hers. Taking my hand and putting it to her ass, I smirked at the sudden interest. Alaya had taken the hint and given us some privacy causing Lem to laugh. "How long?"

"Just a few hours at the most, baby."

Grabbing my hand as we traveled upstairs, she looked back at me with that look in her eyes. Arriving to the closest room, which just so happened to be one of the guest bathrooms, she'd pulled me inside and shut the door behind us.

We'd both fumbled with our clothes, but luckily, she was wearing a dress around the house for the day. Bending over and arching her back, taking in her entirety, I placed a kiss on her back and got down on my knees, feasting upon her sweetness. With accuracy and precision, my tongue licked every crevice, darting in every way possible as she moaned out. I cut on the water to drown out her moans.

"Ooohhh shit," she moaned, her voice barely above a whisper. "I want it. I want it now."

Taking kindly to her desperation, it turned me on as she hopped onto the counter as I widened her legs. Crashing her lips to mine, she started to stroke my growing erection as she positioned it at her opening. Moaning into my mouth, her tongue slipped inside of it. This initiated in us sloppily tonguing one another down as if our lives had depended on this moment.

Taking my time and getting her all juiced up, our moment was soon ruined by a banging on the bathroom door as she smacked her lips. Staying inside of her warm wetness, we paused as she managed to catch her breath.

"Yaz, nigga, come on, fuck!" Trevan fussed.

"A'ight nigga, gimme a minute!"

"A minute?" Lemy repeated. "Nah nigga, you not about to quick nut my ass and then leave, fuck that!"

"What?" Moving inside of her, she started to say something else, but it was replaced by nothing as she bit her bottom lip and closed her eyes. "Yea, talk that shit now. What you were saying?"

"N-nothing, I wasn't saying nothing." Shaking her head and unable to control herself, I continued to talk my shit, noticing her holding back.

"Who is this for?"

"You baby, all you!"

"What?"

"Yasir, don't stop. Please, baby, don't stop!"

Putting in much-needed work, she held out for much longer than I'd thought, but once her legs began to shake, it was over. Climaxing simultaneously, I stayed inside of her while turning off the faucet.

"Lemme turn on the shower so that we can get cleaned up."

"No," she whined. Pecking her lips a single time and turning on the shower, I pulled her down as we started another round.

❧

"Sir, do you have a minute to spare?"

Removing my glasses and meeting Chev at the door, Detective Paul was at his side as I scoffed, not in the mood for no bullshit ass games with this nigga. No matter where I turned or how I moved, he was always sniffing around in shit that had nothing to do with him, and his presence irritated me.

"We can take this outside. My wife and daughter are resting. So, y'all can follow me."

With Christmas being days away, the Louisiana weather had switched to a cold front just in time for the holidays. Chev had given Paul and I some privacy as we'd occupied the lounge chairs on our patio.

"What seems to be the problem now, Detective?"

"I'm just gonna cut to the chase. Are you familiar with a man by the name of Zurich Carter?"

"Nah, that name doesn't ring a bell. Why do you ask?"

"Maybe this will help." Opening the folder he'd held, he removed a picture. As I took it, I immediately got pissed. Staring at the same nigga who I'd caught Lem with, I held a poker face and shrugged.

"Nah."

"That's too bad because he was recently killed."

Revealing more pictures of his bloody demise, I didn't feel no type of way. Niggas died every day, so I couldn't seem to understand what had made this nigga so special.

"You're right, that is too bad. Excuse my language, but what the fuck that gotta do with me?"

"Witnesses were brought in with different statements and your wife is a primary suspect. I'm not pointing any fingers, but various people have reported having seen her meeting up with him some time ago. For what reason, you may need to ask your wife, and in the meantime, she'll probably need a lawyer as well."

"So you trying to put this shit on my wife? You and whoever these bullshit ass witnesses are fools. I should've known yo ass was coming in here with some bullshit. You can see yourself out, my man."

Chapter Twenty-Eight

LEMY

"Is she okay?"

"She just doing that shit because her damn father is not here. She'll be alright. Just ignore her, she'll eventually cry herself to sleep."

I probably sounded like one of those mothers who didn't give a fuck about their child, but this migraine and my current feeling like shit while trying to pretend as if I were okay was slowly starting to cause me to crack under pressure.

"I don't know if this pregnancy is making you mean, but you need to tone it down."

Not even Milan's half-assed gestures to keep my ass calm were working, because everything was pissing me off. Along with this new pregnancy, I also was feeling guilty as fuck for still lying to my man, especially with this huge ass void weighing on me.

Refusing to watch the news for any reports of Zurich's death, I somehow knew I was going to need to come to clean to Yaz soon. Not knowing how he'd handle the news once I'd revealed everything to him, I suppose a part of me was protecting him from the horrific truth about the person he called his mother.

Christmas was days away, but despite the most joyous time of the year, shit was ultimately about to hit the fan.

"The quicker we find out who did this to him, the quicker we can move the fuck on with our lives. You know that. That bitch ain't got shit on you. Look at how you're living, Lemy. She's just jealous and bitches like that will never move anywhere in the world."

"It's not remotely the same when you know what the fuck we're up against. It's not like back then, Milan. I got a damn daughter and a baby on the way to think about! I can't just do whatever I please anymore, everything I do has to be for the sake of my family, and I'm sorry, but maybe if you had a nigga, then you'd know how I fuckin' feel."

Realizing I'd come off a bit harsh, it was far too late as I sighed, watching her grab her shit and begin to shake her head.

"You know what bitch, fuck you because I've always had your back. Don't think just because this nigga got you living lavishly that you can shit on who always been down for you! As a matter of fact, I feel fuckin' bad for Yaz, because you ain't did shit but fuck up his life since the moment he's met you."

"Excuse me? This must be how you really been feeling from the jump, huh?" I questioned. "Well, bitch, keep that same ass energy when you need me. Who the fuck been on your side when yo ass didn't have shit to your name, huh? You know what? Fuck you, Milan. I don't need a jealous bitch like you telling me shit about what the fuck I got going on, so fuck you."

"You gonna need me more than I need you, that's a promise."

"Get the fuck outta my shit, did I fuckin' stutter?"

Milan and I have had some fair share of disagreements. This one just like the others would go down, yet within the next few days, we'd be back joined at the hip as if nothing happened between us.

Truth be told, never in life has a situation ever had me this fucked up like this one did. I didn't know whether it was that I had children to think about or what, but the nightmares are every damn night to the point where I barely rest comfortably throughout the night. Every single time it's the same thing— my entire family being killed right before my eyes and lastly, this baby perishing as well. The pain is so realistic and excruciating to the point where I'm popping up like the shit is real.

As fucked as it may sound, I felt like this was my own karma for all the shit I've done in my past. Snapping out of my trance, Yaz entered our home looking like he had a pretty shitty day himself. I could see the exhaustion expressed all over his face as Yara's crying caused him to make his way over to the kitchen.

"What's wrong with daddy's baby, huh? Stop crying, Dudi." Wiping away her tears, his small smile fainted as he turned to me. "I need to talk to you."

"About?" Yara's sounds immediately diminished as he began to rock her to sleep.

"Is there something you need to tell me?" His stare and the seriousness of his tone was intimidating, menacing almost as I shrugged nervously. "Ya know, I just wish you'd be honest with me. Why can I never get that from you?"

"I'm not with the mind games, Ya and I'm really not in the mood, so please just tell me-"

"That nigga I caught you with, he dead or did you already know?"

Maintaining my poker face, he awaited for a response, as I said nothing, afraid I may say the wrong thing.

"Well, since you acting like you'on know what the fuck I'm talking about, I'ma just be straight up. Did you do it?"

"I'm getting real tired of you asking me shit like this. You know me. Yes, I have a past, but I'm not that fuckin' dumb, Yaz."

"So you did know," he stated, answering his own question. "And for the record, what else am I supposed to think, huh? Every single time I ask you some shit, you either lying or betraying me."

"I'm not that type of woman anymore, and you know that."

"No, I don't know that, Halima. I don't and you wanna know why because I feel like I can't trust my own damn wife. For all I know, you could've been behind that shit with my mama. What's to say I'm not right about that?"

"So, I'm just this ghetto, crazy ass bitch going around just killing everybody, huh? If you actually opened up your fuckin' eyes Yasir, you'd know everything I've done was to protect you!"

Keeping his mouth closed, he didn't say a single word and just began to walk away. I needed a breather, so I refused to chase behind him. I was forever chasing behind his ass, but I wasn't his mama, and he'd unfortunately grown so used to his bitch ass mama babying him all the damn time that he didn't even realize it was causing a distance between us.

Yasir was spoiled, so whenever he didn't want to face the facts regarding something, he'd run away. He's done it more times than once, and he'll do it again. I was a lot of things, but being stupid enough to raise a man wasn't about to be added onto the list of those things.

"Go ahead and run the fuck away like you always do! How you gonna start some shit then run off? And I know you're not ignoring me!"

I'd just about had it up to here with the bullshit, and I'd reached my limit. I've been way too nice to this nigga, and I was damn tired of being treated like shit by him, his stupid ass mama and all the bullshit that comes along with him and the unwanted ass drama.

"Give me my fuckin' keys, man."

"Fuck you and these damn keys, nigga!" I shouted, throwing them elsewhere. "You're gonna just walk the fuck away like you always do, right? Grow the fuck up, Yasir and be a fuckin' man about yo shit! What, you running to yo stupid ass mama, ain't you? Ain't you?"

"You wanna talk shit about protection," he shot back, catching me completely off guard as I backed into the staircase. "Protection is saving yo dumb ass from being a prime suspect in a murder investigation, that's protection! You're quick to say a nigga never had yo fuckin' back when I'm always cleaning up bullshit you created and fucked up!"

Chastising me with his words, I couldn't even respond to him. Usually, my rebuttals would be spoken in a millisecond, but this time, he told no lies. Maybe Milan was right. Maybe Gen B was right, and maybe, just maybe everyone was right about me. Ever since the day I've entered this man's life, I've created nothing but turmoil, and I don't know whether the emotions from this pregnancy had me on edge or what but something needed to shake.

"Don't," I mustered out, stopping him from comforting me. Tears spilled from my eyes as I angrily wiped them away.

"Come here, tell me what's wrong."

"I can't."

"You can, and you will."

"Baby, I can't," I whispered. "I don't wanna hurt you. I can't see you hurt. You have to trust me, please."

"Okay, okay, I trust you, baby," he whispered as I turned to him. "I trust you, and we're gonna get through this. I promise you."

Chapter Twenty-Nine

YAZ

"I sure do hate to see you all go. It's breaking the ole man's heart."

"I'm just doing what I was taught to do, pops."

Instead of doing the usual opening of presents and just basking in the holiday spirit, our home was filled with boxes as moving vans occupied our front lawn working diligently to properly assist with a proper moving. To me, there was no much better time than today, and although it hurt to leave our beloved city, it was officially time for a new start.

"I'm proud of you, son. I wish I had the mindset like yours back when I was this age. So, the new house is a go?"

"Not yet, the big things like furniture and unnecessary miscellaneous shit are going into storage until the house is complete. But for now, we staying at the beach house, which is more than enough space, especially with the baby coming."

Truth be told, this move was much more than a new start, but we were ultimately leaving behind the bullshit this year had brought about. For the first time, I was doing what Yaz wanted and right now, that was focusing on the well-being of my family.

"When you gonna tell your mother?"

"Once we're long gone. I figure it's best to do this while every-body's preoccupied anyway."

"Well, like I said, I'm giving you at least a good three months off to get your shit together, but once that happens, I expect to see you not missing a damn thing." Preaching some words of wisdom, I took it all in. I could tell it pained him to see us go, but I was doing what was best for all of us.

"Traveling won't be an issue. It's just gonna be harder on Lem with the back and forth, but she's a tough woman, and she can handle it."

"No woman can handle pregnancy all while raising a toddler on her own, Yasir. Take it from me. Shit, at least you had enough of sense to get one woman pregnant and not two. I'm glad you dodged that bullet."

"Everybody can't be a Dara Cosart, huh ole man?"

"Yea, yea keep on talking that shit. When's the last time you spoke to your mother?"

"We talked earlier, but it wasn't for long. She kept asking about this case on this dude and shit, but it'll be best if she didn't know any details."

"How the hell does she even know about this shit if it concerns only Lemy?"

"Yo guess just as good as mine, which is even more of a reason as to why I need to get the entire fuck, excuse my language. Don't get me wrong, I love mama with everything in me, I do, but seeing her true colors and shit just got me wondering."

"Always follow your gut like I told you."

"Can I ask you a serious question?" Switching gears and taking a break from taping up boxes, I'd taken a sip from my iced water.

"Go ahead, what's on your mind?"

"What type of past did mama have before me?"

"All I know is that she had a few run-ins with the law way before you were even thought about. She didn't tell me much, because well, I didn't too much care to know. However, when we met, she was running away from some cat she had a past with. I always forget his name, but the story is as ancient as fuckin' hell."

"Mama doesn't seem like the type to run away from nobody."

"You'on know your mama like I do." He laughed, shaking his head. "No, no boy, you'on know her."

"Well, how about you tell me some stories over a good ole hot sausage po-boy?"

"Now you're speaking my language!"

Heading upstairs, Lemy was sleeping, which damn near seemed to be her new hobby. Thankfully, Yara was spending some last minute time with Alaya, Trevan, and My Dear before we took off. Plus, I could tell Lem had needed the extra rest, due to her restless nights and current nightmares.

"Baby?" Kissing her shoulder as she lightly snored, I kissed her lips as she squirmed and began to open her eyes.

"What time is it?"

"It's only two, you good. I spoke to Lay Lay, and Du is doing good. She gonna bring her tonight. I'ma head out for a minute with pops. Rozman is gonna be at the gate, and I'm leaving Chev, too."

"Okay baby, go enjoy time with your dad. I love you."

"I love you, too."

"No, no," she whined, pulling my face to hers. "You know better than to leave here without kissing me. Bring that ass here."

Meeting her halfway, I brought my lips to hers, and they moved in an undeniable sync. Damn near getting carried away, she giggled and pulled away, then pecked them a single time. Grazing her thumb across my lip line, she yawned and laid back as I tucked her in while bending down to kiss her stomach.

"You better be up when I get back."

"I'll try."

Arriving at one of our favorite spots, Gene's, luckily the establishment had opened on the holiday, and we were currently enjoying the delicious goodness. Wiping mayo from my mouth and taking a sip from my Dr. Pepper, pops started to laugh.

"What the fuck is so funny, man?"

"You honestly think yo ass is gonna be able to let go of this good ass food for that Florida bullshit? I give yo ass about a good month or two before you start missing home."

"I ain't gonna even lie to you, I'ma miss my city, but it's not just about me. I got babies depending on me, one here already and another one on the way. Plus, Lem ain't never really had no real family to depend on," I admitted. "With this shit with mama and all this other drama, I can't put her through no more of that, man. I already put her through far worst, and she deserves better."

"I'll tell you like I said once before, that woman is one of a kind, and she's different. You won't find too many like her."

"So, you think I'm doing the right thing?"

"I'll never steer you in the wrong direction, son. You're a Cosart. We may make a few mistakes, but we'll always do whatever is needed to right whatever wrongs we've created. I raised you to become a man who knows his right from wrong. You're not no dumb nigga."

"Shit, with the way Lem call me outta my damn name, I'm starting to think dumb and stupid nigga should have been my damn name."

Touching base with pops is just what the doctored had ordered, especially since this would probably be the last time that we'd seen each other for a minute. Unlike the bond I'd shared with mama, my pops was a loyal one. I remember as a younger dude, I'd always do the absolute best in sports and academics, just to see that smile on his face and it worked every single time.

"Damn, lemme call and check on Lem." Pulling out my phone to see three missed calls from her, I frowned and called back, only to get her voicemail.

"You okay?"

"Lem's not answering her phone. You got yours on you?"

"That shit died an hour ago."

"Something is not right." Trying Chev and Roz's phone, their phones did the same thing, sparking an immediate sense of urgency as I shook my head. "We gotta dip."

"Lead the way."

Chapter Thirty

LEMY

"Damn it. I should've brought my damn charger."

Seated in the Audi parked in front of Milan's home, I noticed her Benz in the lot, which meant she was home. I contemplated whether I wanted to go in or not. Placing my dead phone into my purse, I knew I'd have to deal with Yaz's mouth once I returned home.

Before meeting Yaz, Milan was the only family I'd had. We'd always be joined at the hip. We've gone through our fair share of disagreements, but my emotions have been all over the place, and I felt like I needed my girl right now, especially since this would be my last few days in our hometown.

"Milan?"

Using my spare key and removing my Chanel slides, I shut the door behind me and turned on the light, only for it not to come on. Trying it for the second time, the light did the same thing. Venturing further inside and ignoring all the possible signs that I needed to turn my ass around, the front door soon slammed shut as I turned around.

"Milan ain't here," the voice matched the face as Jhea stood with a gun in her hands as she turned on the lights. Her menacing smile and laugh matched the devious stare as she began to try her best to intimidate me.

"It's about damn time you grew some balls and finally stepped to me. Silly me for thinking yo dumb ass was acting alone, once a sneaky bitch, always a sneaky ass bitch, right?"

"It takes one to know one, my good sis. I never meant for it to get this bad. Milan was just too damn in the middle of shit all the fuckin' time and you, you just never were satisfied with the fact that a nigga was just using yo stupid ass."

"Using me?" I repeated, cocking my eyebrow with a stifled laugh. "That nigga loved me, and you couldn't stand it, Jhea. You were so jealous that I had him in ways you never could, so you went behind my back. Even then, it was still not enough for you. That nigga is dead and gone, yet the shit still fucks with you, so who's really the stupid one?"

"You know I'm getting real fuckin' tired of you thinking you the shit, bitch!" With the gun now turned on me, I had not an ounce of fear in my heart. If she really were going to shoot, she would've done the shit a long time ago.

Not too much caring about her next move, I sensed another presence. Low and behold, Gen B joined her with a menacing smile as well. Blood coated her attire as my mind immediately went to Milan's safety because you never really knew with two stupid ass bitches thinking they were running shit.

"What, cat got your tongue?" Gen B questioned. "Why are you looking so shocked?"

"I feel so damn bad for Yasir, I really fuckin' do."

"And you wanna know what, if it weren't for you, this could've gone much differently than it did."

"The fuck is that supposed to mean?"

The sound of screeching tires managed to catch our attention as I prayed to God that Yaz wasn't stupid enough to fall for any of this. Jhea approached me. Pointing the gun at me and pushing it at my temple, she forced me onto the ground. Once the door had opened, it was entirely too late, Yaz stood confused not knowing he'd walked into a twisted ass web of turmoil.

Before he could even open his mouth, a shot was fired hitting Yaz.

I screamed, stunned at the fact that Gen B had the gall to shoot her own son.

"You fuckin' crazy ass bitch!" I screamed, turning to him. "Yaz, baby, are you okay? Yasir!"

"Jhea, go get the chair so that we can tie these two up."

"You sure?"

"Yea, she ain't going nowhere, and neither is he." Speaking as if she had no heart whatsoever, Jhea followed the directions from her puppet master as I shook my head.

Yaz didn't move, and the more time passed, the more frightened I'd become. He'd flinched and started to move, pulling himself up, and holding the wound on his stomach. Unable to speak, his eyes met mine.

"He's going to fuckin' bleed out, do something!" An emotionless Gen B, stood holding the gun to me as she sat on the sectional, making herself comfortable. "What the fuck is wrong with you? Are you really gonna let your son fuckin' die? How stupid can you be?"

"Just as stupid as he is once he believed I'd be okay with this bull-shit you caused!"

"Bullshit? Bitch, the hot ass bullshit is the shit you've done to turn him against me. Let's fuckin' get into it! When were you gonna tell him about his real father?" Talking my shit, she sat there shocked by what had come out of my mouth as I nodded, having her right where I wanted her. "Yea, you can't say shit now, can you? Yaz, she's been lying to you your entire life baby. I swear I wanted to protect you."

His eyes were full of confusion as he shook his head, staring between us.

"Don't you listen to her, Yazzy," she cooed, joining him. Reaching out to caress his face, he shook his head and moved away from her. "Mama's done all she can to protect you. This bitch wouldn't know the first thing about protection even if it slapped her in the damn face!"

"It was you, wasn't it? You're the witness putting this shit on her?"

"I needed you to see her true colors, son I—"

"This coming from the woman who just shot her fuckin' son!" Stunned by the fact that he'd even raised his voice at her, she didn't say a word as she began to cry out. This Oscar performance was so phony to the point where I actually did hurt for her because this bitch was crazier than I'd thought.

"Tell me the truth, mama. That's all I ask. Is any of this she's saying true?"

"Yazzy, baby I'm so sorry."

"Come on, man," he expressed, shaking his head. "You call this protecting me? How the fuck are you gonna lie to me my whole life? My whole life a fuckin' lie! I wanted so bad to give you the benefit of the doubt, but look at how you do me and for what?"

"This is all her fault!" she shouted, pointing the gun at me. "She turned you against me! I've tried everything. I even went as far as bringing Brielle back just for you two to rekindle things, Yazzy. She loves you so much!"

"Shut the fuck up! You sound fuckin' crazy. This has nothing to with Lemy!"

"Yasir, be careful," I pleaded.

"You stay outta this! You know what? Fuck this! You lil' ungrateful bastard, I sacrificed everything for you, everything! But you're too weak to even realize how much I've done for you, all my life Yasir!"

"I didn't ask you for none of that!"

Slapping the butt of the gun across his face, she fucked up once she'd turned her back as I picked up the closest thing to me, which was a vase and smashed it against her head. Falling to the ground, the gun had fallen from her hands as I rushed to Yaz's side, while tucking the gun away in my jeans.

Disoriented, I checked his wound as more blood continued to gush from it as I applied pressure, resulting in him screaming with labored breathing.

"Shhhh, shhh, it's gonna be okay. Just keep pressure on it," I whispered, taking off my sweater and pressing it against the bleeding. Wincing, I held his hand as he tried to speak as I shook my head. "No, don't talk. I'll be back. I'm gonna get us outta here. Okay?"

"I...love you."

"I love you too, baby, so much." Kissing his lips, I knew I didn't have too much time before Jhea returned.

Traveling upstairs as quietly as possible, I entered Milan's room and had to cover my mouth from screaming as tears filled my eyes. Sobbing into my hand, she was laid in a pool of her own blood. Gashes and lacerations were all over her body as I moved closer, seeing the visible cut on her neck.

Searching for a phone, I yanked Milan's from the charger and immediately called 911. Damn near like déjà vu. This was almost similar to the same ass situation I'd found myself in last year.

"9-1-1, what is your emergency?"

"Yes, I need a medic and the police immediately. Please hurry."

"Ma'am, help is on the—"

Screaming out, the pain was so great that it knocked the wind out of me. I'd fallen to the ground holding my stomach, seeing a knife lodged into my side. Turning over, a powerful kick was delivered to my side, pushing the knife even further, followed by another one as I yanked it out. Jhea stood over me.

"I never thought it'd come to this, sis."

"You want my life so bad. Bitch, you could never be me on your worst day hoe! Now that I think about it, Hasaan would be ashamed of you. I had that nigga in ways you never could, and it fuckin' kills you!"

"You had him alright, Lemy. You did, I give you that, but at least I was smart enough to move differently! You think just because you done scammed on a rich nigga you living it up, bitch? I feel bad for you and that bastard ass baby!"

"She's not for Hasaan, Jhea! I don't know what the fuck Indie might've told you, but he had it all wrong. Yes, I killed Hasaan, and he deserved every ounce of that shit, but we got our own beef. Why the fuck would you team up with an old hoe to settle something like this?"

"Your mother-in-law a real hood bitch. She came to me, and everything was all her. Everything worked out so perfectly. Hell, she even got that Brielle bitch to get back with your new nigga. She whipped that pussy on that ass so good and got the nigga right back on that shit." She laughed, shaking her head.

"I never knew a mother could be so fucked up 'til I met her, but she was willing to do anything to get'chu outta the picture. Zurich was collateral, just as well as Milan. Well, I wanted to tag along because I'm sick and tired of you. If I can oust one Hodge, I might as well get rid of the other one."

"That'll never happen, even in the afterlife. Bitch, you'll wish you never fucked with me. Do me a favor and kiss Hasaan for me."

Looking confused, I grabbed the gun and squeezed the trigger as the bullet pierced her chest. As she hit the floor, I struggled and stood to my feet, firing off more shots into her body until there were no more bullets.

"The both of y'all sick fucks can kiss my fuckin' ass now, bitch!" Spitting on her, I dropped the gun and checked her pockets, retrieving another gun full of bullets as I shook my head. "Stupid, duck ass bitch."

The sound of sirens in the distance made me feel a tad bit better as I rushed downstairs to Yaz's side. Gen B was still on the ground. I noticed how pale Yaz was beginning to look as he opened eyes with a weakened smile. Intertwining his blood covered hands into mines, I kissed his forehead as he began to cough.

"They're almost here, baby. You have to hold on." Opening his mouth to speak, his breathing began to quicken as I sniffled, the grip he had on my hands becoming weaker. "Yaz, baby, please hold on. Stay up for me, please."

"I'm cold, why is it so...cold?"

Gen B moved, her whole entire body twitching as I watched her get up and stand to her feet, completely disoriented as she smiled.

"Don't make me fuckin' do this, I'm begging you. If you had any sense, you'd walk away!"

"If I can't have him, then you can't either."

As Gen B charged at me, I fired off two shots, and she fell to the ground. Dropping the gun, I held Yaz's face. As his eyes began to close, the paramedics burst through the door and began to take over.

Chapter Thirty-One

LEMY

Nine Months Later

Strength and wisdom were the qualities my late mother said every woman needed, but as a young girl, I could never understand why she'd constantly instill those two essential words into our minds.

I could easily remember Aneema and I being so damn confused when mama would sit us down for her little heart to heart talks. Every single sit-down was always better than the next, so I kept them close knowing eventually that those simple talks would help me in the long run.

Nothing in this world could amount up to the pain of having those loved ones you cared about so deeply to be snatched away without you even getting the chance to say goodbye. They always did say the third time was a charm, but I never did see myself overcoming any of these obstacles I've overcome without mama, Aneema, and Milan at my side. In essence, I'd like to say their absence happened because there were other things in store for me.

Cradling my newest blessing, I had given birth to this sweet, baby boy. He was everything my weeping heart needed and more. Yasin was the missing piece to the puzzle that I've so long ago needed to complete, and now that he was physically here, it was time to begin a newer journey with finally accepting that family is constant and forever.

Even in my darkest days, my strength refused to falter or wither knowing I had Yara and Yasin depending on me.

Relocating to Florida was, for the most part, the hardest thing I'd ever had to endure, but leaving behind those terrible memories in New Orleans is what was needed for a proper resetting on everything.

"I hope you're not burning no shit up in my new ass kitchen, nigga."

Bouncing back like the Superman that he is, on that night, I thought I'd lost my sanctuary and sanity. Luckily, Yaz pushed through and was only left with a nasty scar to remind of us all we'd endured on that horrific night.

Shirtless, I'd ran my fingers across the scar and stood on my tiptoes, kissing his lips as he squeezed my ass and playfully bit down onto my bottom lip.

"Why you always gotta rib a nigga?"

"Because I know you won't do shit, but talk yo shit. How was work, today?"

"Same ole shit, but the first phase of construction for the Florida location started today. I hate seeing my pops still working and shit, so I told him to retire. The only thing is that I'ma be gone more than usual, but I know you can handle it."

"I'm a big girl, but that still won't do shit for me missing you all hours of the day."

"You miss me even when I'm in the next room, Lem."

"Okay, and I can do that because I'm your fuckin' wife," I stated proudly. "I spoke to the pediatric audiologist, and Sin's hearing aid should be here in no time. How you feel about that?"

"Well, at least my son is gonna be finally able to fully hear me, so I'm happy for that. I just hate he gotta go through that shit, ya know."

Another sensitive topic we hated discussing was discovering our baby boy was completely deaf in his right ear. Doctors say that sometimes some things tend to happen in the womb that nobody can control, but I already know it had everything to do with what took place on that night.

Yaz and I have moved past everything, but it still hurt to this very day. Some nights I still struggled with sleeping to the point where he mentioned seeing a therapist, but I'd much rather deal with my own shit without the likes of a professional. I tend to look at this way. Everything was now in the past and focusing on our future was all that mattered, especially since we were both in such good spirits with no likes of any drama.

"It could be much worse, baby. We just gotta deal with the cards we're dealt." I shrugged.

"Yea, you're right and since we on the topic of this shit. I still think you should talk to that therapist. You ain't been sleeping in days, Halima."

"Okay, you seem to have fuckin' forget that I got a one-year-old and a two-month-old to care for now when you're working. Don't start. I don't wanna talk about any of that tonight."

"I'm not trying to piss you off, I just wanna help, and I can't do that if you're shutting me out."

"Answer your phone, Yasir."

I was a gutta bitch, and whatever problems within myself that I did have were going to be handled personally. These few lessons thrown at me didn't do a damn thing except trained me up to be even more mindful and cold-hearted whenever it comes down to these hating ass bitches. Some old shit just doesn't tend to die down, and whether you liked it or not, it was up to you to nip it in the bud or cancel out the enemy all on your own.

Hell, this shit was my life.

Every day that I looked at my reflection, I thank the higher power that I didn't look like any of the shit I've been through. At the end of the day, it's always been just me. Loyalty was everything, and my true real ones are watching me, guiding me, and are damn impressed by what Little Miss Lemy was capable of when being thrown against all fuck shit. All my life this demon ass bad luck has ridden my ass through and through until I finally got tired of becoming a victim and decided to do something about the shit.

Snapping away from my thoughts, the baby monitor began to go off, erupting with Yasin's helpless whimpers. As a mother, you knew when your child was in danger, and the unfamiliar sound grabbed my attention as I sped upstairs, pushing all negative thoughts out of my mind.

Entering his bedroom, I was relieved only to see that he was perfectly fine. Scooping him up in my arms, he started to fuss while sucking his fingers as a breeze of fresh air coming from his window crept into the room. Carefully rocking him, his light brown eyes stared into mine, causing my heart to warm at how handsome he was.

"It's okay, baby boy. Mommy's right here."

Like his sister, he'd taken after his father with a strong resemblance. Every single vivid detail Yasir had was passed down to his first son. It was the ultimate betrayal carrying your children full term only for each of them to come out looking like their father, but it was a different type of betrayal.

Drifting off to sleep, I carefully placed him into his crib and closed the window, locking it as well.

Exiting and stepping across the hall to Yara's room, she turned to the door wide-awake as I laughed. She might've been her father's twin, but that attitude and her ways were all me.

"Why are you still up, little girl?" Sitting on the edge of her bed, she pointed to the window, which was also open. I sighed. "Mommy's gonna get daddy for leaving this open. Come here, what's wrong, baby girl?"

Yawning, she rubbed her eyes and laid onto my chest. Staying at her side until she'd fallen asleep, I'd tucked her in and leaned over, shutting and locking her window. Before leaving, I bent down and pressed my lips to her cheek and left a little crack in her door and traveled back downstairs to the kitchen.

"I wish you'd stop leaving them fuckin' windows open, especially in Yara's room. She's walking now, and she's known for getting into shit, so when you're on daddy duty, don't forget to lock and close them."

"I ain't leave no fuckin' window open." Scrunching up his face, I rolled my eyes and nodded. "What?"

"Yea, yea, whatever. I know I didn't do it, so who else was it? The damn ghost?"

"You blowing this shit outta proportion like always. Calm yo ass down before I bend you over this table and fuck that attitude outta you."

A sudden throbbing between my legs had immediately begun as I sauntered over to him. Geared up and ready, he aggressively pulled me onto his lap as I crashed my lips to his.

Slapping my ass followed by a vice grip, food was no longer on my mind as he pulled back.

"Wait, wait." He sighed, complete seriousness in his tone.

"Whatever it is, it can't wait?"

"No, it can't, that was the facility calling me. It's about mama."

"What, they can't fuckin' control her ass? If that's the case, I'on really see the point in you shelling out all this damn money for a five-star ass mental health place, only for her to still be making shit difficult."

Gen B, similar to all fucked up shit in my life, was still a sensitive topic that we rarely touched on. On that night, when I was given the opportunity to shoot, I didn't. Something within me was tugging at the strings of my heart saying that I needed to move on and eventually do the right thing.

When I did shoot, I only grazed her mainly because, at the end of the day, she was still the woman who'd given birth to my everything. Killing her would've caused so much bullshit neither one of us needed, so to avoid any more difficulties with moving forward as one, I spared her life. Yaz had managed to get her in with some of the best mental health professionals, where she was soon diagnosed with schizophrenia and being bipolar.

"No babe, that's not it."

"Then what the fuck is it? Are you moving her again?"

"No Halima, they can't find her. Her doctor was on the phone, and she...he went in for the routine checkup, and she wasn't there. They think she might've broken out."

EPILOGUE

"How many nights will you be staying, ma'am?" The young receptionist had been on his phone throughout his entire shift, completely unbeknownst to news reports of a severely dangerous patient escaping from a mental health facility.

Gen B was a pro at staying under the radar. With many aliases under her belt, merely disappearing without a trace was one of the many things she was good at. As night had fallen, the small skies were scattered with stars as she stared out her window in deep thought on how she'd lost everything she'd work so hard for.

The ultimate plan was to officially rid Lemy out of Yaz's life for good, but once the babies were thrown into the mix, she was side-tracked. Not only did this sorry excuse of a woman entered their lives at full force, but she'd done the unthinkable with blessing Gen B's darkened heart with not only, but two grandchildren— a beautiful girl and handsome boy.

For years, she'd spent her whole life bettering all harsh realities and situations in preparation for her one and only, her son to become the most prominent man in the city. Biologically, ever since discovering herself to be pregnant, she'd known from that day forward she'd have to protect him by all means.

Over the years, she stood closely and at his side, observing him to grow into becoming much more of a man than his biological father.

Don Carter and Gen B were a force. She'd come from absolutely nothing, so leaching onto a big name seemed to be the answer to all her problems. Despite wanting nothing except the reputation that'd come along with becoming attached a big name, she remained at Don's side until her life slowly began to look up from her poverty-stricken past.

Every woman had envied how much of a hold Gen B had on Don, but everyone had also known she was his one and only. No matter how fucked up her ways had been, she would go to earth's end to assure all negativity skipped right over the love of her life.

Behind closed doors, everything that glittered wasn't gold. To everyone on the outside looking in, Don and Gen B were a match made in heaven. They sported the finest labels, rode in the finest cars, and stayed in the biggest house to whereas the city often looked to them as hood royalty.

Aside from all the glorious things, Don's jealousy happened to be a thing neither one of them could escape. Mentally, he struggled with depression, and it'd only come to the surface while he was under some type of stress. The abuse began with words, suddenly transpiring into his fist being the only thing to keep his woman on the right track. You see, Gen B had been fucked up way before Don had even done more damage.

The two loved each other deeply but couldn't seem to see their lives functioning properly without one another. Years down the line, due to the stress and abuse, Gen struggled mentally and physically with bearing a child full term. After countless miscarriages and two stillbirths, upon discovering herself to be pregnant, she immediately knew she had to do all in her power to protect her child from the monster Don was beginning to grow into.

Pouring rain erupting from outside had fallen onto the home Don had shared with Gen as she sat awaiting her man's arrival. Late nights were a thing all future wives of kingpins got used to, especially since Don's rise to prominence and notoriety was beginning to come in between their relationship.

Ignoring the crazed voices in her head, she soon disappeared into the bath-

room as the darkened purplish bruises reflected in the mirror. In her mind, love had meant enduring all things needed to keep him close and satisfied. It was the one thing her disheveled mother had instilled within her ever since she was a little girl.

"Vie!" Don's voice erupted throughout their home, followed by the slamming of the door. "Woman, where you at?"

"I've been waiting on you," escaped her lips in a voice barely above a whisper, she stood stunned at the gentleman standing at Don's side. He was handsome, extremely handsome, and although Don was everything to her, she forced a smile as she approached the two men standing before here.

"Sweetheart, this is my old friend I've told you about. Meet the entrepreneur, Dara Cosart. Dara, I'd like for you to meet my lady love, Genevie."

"Nice to finally meet the woman this one can't seem to stop talking about," Dara stated warmly.

"I sure do hope they were good things. Usually, Don never brings his work home with him. I sure do hope this is extremely important."

In the streets, it was very seldom for a woman to be informed on anything pertaining to their man's business. Deep down, Don's blood was boiling because once again, Gen was speaking out of turn, which was immediate disrespect in his eyes.

§☙

Hours after Dara had left, Don warped into the monster that Gen had become frightened of over time. Due to the storm, the power had gone out, and the only light source throughout the room was coming from the candles he'd lit as he delivered numerous kicks, punches, and all forceful blows onto her frail body as if she were an animal.

"Bitch, I tell you time after time to stay outta my business? Do I not?"

Sending another kick to her body as she laid curled in a fetal position, he'd wiped the sweat from his forehead and pointed towards her. "If I gotta beat the fuck outta you every night to straighten you out, then that's what the fuck I'ma do until you learn to never fix your mouth about any of my business. Do I make myself clear?"

"I'm sorry. I'm so sorry!"

"Save your sorry ass excuses for somebody who wanna hear it. Clean your-self up!"

Exiting the room, the lights soon powered themselves back on. As she strug-gled to pull herself up from the floor, she prayed to God that he'd spared the life of the child forming inside of her womb.

Don had known of her pregnancy but ultimately saw the child as a threat with coming in between the intense love he had for his woman and the impor-tance of his thriving business. In his eyes, a child was not a thing besides collat-eral to be used against him when caught in the midst of crossfire.

Following the orders of her lover, she soaked in a bathtub, the clear water soon darkening due to the blood seeping from her wounds. Her belly, at five months, wasn't as large as it should've been, but the child was indeed a miracle and would soon be the solution needed to the life she deserved.

Snapping out her deep trance, an avid knocking on the door erupted as Gen B securely reached for her gun. Not expecting any visi-tors, she removed the safety and peeped through the peephole, her heart rambunctiously beating as Dara stood on the other side.

Opening the door, the two shared an embrace as she broke down into a full-blown sob.

What started as a friendship soon blossomed into something more. Ever since first laying eyes on him, she'd known this man would grow with becoming not only one of her greatest, dearest friends but also the love of her life.

"How'd you know where to find me?" Breaking the silence, Dara thumbed away his tears and grabbed her hands.

"Genevie, I'll always know where you are. I can't begin to imagine how this all may seem to you, but sweetheart, you know this isn't where you need to be."

"Don't come here trying to persuade me!" Gen voiced, defensively standing to her feet.

Even at her lowest, Dara still loved her immensely. Despite her mental illnesses and everything she'd put him through, he just couldn't completely turn his back on the broken woman who'd captured his heart.

Accepting her flaws and all was a big step for any man, but Dara saw it as a blessing in disguise. Assisting her to finally leave Don is a task he'll forever be grateful for completing, because not only did he win the woman, but Dara also won the child, who would soon grow up and look to him for guidance was the bonus he couldn't refuse.

"If our son finds out you're here you know this won't end well, my love," he stated, holding her face.

"Genevie, you're sick. You're sick, and he deserves to be happy. He's been through so much. We've put him through so much, and we've done all that we possibly can, but he isn't that little boy anymore. He's a grown ass man with a family of his own, a wife and two children who needs him."

"But I need him more!" she stressed, her voice breaking. "How dare he t-turn his back on me, how dare he! Dara, we can get him back, baby. We can get him back and I can, I can get rid of her. For, for good!"

"No, I won't allow you. I love you so much 'til it hurts, but Genevie I cannot." Standing before her, trying to remain strong, Dara began to break uncontrollably. The door burst open with individuals from the home where she'd escaped as tears streamed down Dara's cheeks.

In his eyes, accepting a broken woman was a task he could handle, but the years the two had spent together had unknowingly taken a toll on him. He loved her so deeply, but he also knew if he didn't step in, then the chances of Yaz to live a stress-free life would be slim to none.

"How could you?" Screaming and fighting against them, he exited the room as Gen B's screams soon died down.

Minutes away from the motel, Yaz laid wide-awake with a sleeping Lemy at his side and two-month-old Yasin, wide-awake cooing and cracking smiles. Yara slept between her mother and father. Despite Lemy's protests, somehow the Cosart children always found their way between their parents almost every single night.

"Put him in his damn crib," Lemy fussed, shielding her eyes. "What the fuck time is it? Why is he still up? Yaz, we've talked about this!"

"Relax," Yaz fussed. "Go yo mean ass back to sleep, man. Don't worry about us."

Carefully standing to his feet with Yasin in his arms, he'd unknow-ingly grown into a family man. Like before, he'd had it all and for once in his life, he was happy to accept the gradual change.

"I'll be so glad once you get older, big man so that you and I can gang up on your mommy and your sister." Yaz smiled. "I know you may not understand much, but just know daddy's gonna do everything in his power to make sure you and your sister live the life I never had."

The ringing of his phone had interrupted the father/son moment as Yaz answered, becoming alarmed seeing Dara calling at such a late hour.

"Pops?" He frowned, cradling Yasin. "What's going on? Why are you calling so late?"

"I found your mother. She was stashed at some hotel a few minutes away from your home, son. Yaz, we're going to need to talk about at least putting her somewhere where she can't escape."

"How was she?"

"She's having another one of her episodes. I know she didn't mean any harm, but you know she's very envious of Lemy right now, so your best bet is to look somewhere further. Understood?"

"Yeah, I hear you. Pops, I just want you to know I appreciate you. I love you, and despite my knowing the truth, you'll always be my father. I want you to know that and we'll work through this."

"I know, son. I love you too. We'll talk more in the morning. Bring my grandchildren along with you, because we have a lot of talking to do."

"I will."

That night, Yaz didn't sleep a wink.

Lemy had known her husband like the back of her hand, and once she left the bathroom, after a well-needed shower, she could see how fatigued he was due to his lack of sleep.

"Another sleepless night, Ya?"

"I just had a lot on my mind." Sitting at his side, she placed herself onto his lap as she brought her lips to his.

"I won't pull it out of you, but we do need to talk whenever you're ready. Okay?"

"A'ight."

Flaws and all, Lemy had loved her husband immensely. Everything she'd spent her life running away from, she soon discovered was all that she truly needed. With her man and her babies at her side, she was unstoppable. It took a lot with realizing you had to initially lose it all to start from the very bottom, and then succeed in all for your life to finally begin to start making any sense.

"Good morning, my daughter," Dara greeted, the two sharing a hug. "Where are my lil' rascals?"

"Yaz is on daddy duty with getting them up, so they should be down soon. I made enough for you. Would you like a plate?"

"Of course, thank you so much."

"Oh whatever, you know you're family."

Dara observed his daughter-in-law, his heart warming at the fact that his son finally found himself a good thing. Like Genevie, Lemy was broken way beyond repair, but he was all for the love exuding from the two seeing as though she'd brought extreme happiness to his son.

"What's good, pops?" Yaz greeted, Yasin in his arms and Yara holding his hand. "Du, go see Papa."

"Good morning, son."

As Dara scooped his granddaughter up in his arms, he'd glanced at the love expressed between the young Cosart's. Throughout all things horrid, their love remained strong, and to him, it was the best thing because it reminded him of happy times shared between himself and Gen B.

Throughout the betrayal, the deceit, the underlying secrets, and the regret, love had overcome it all, resulting in a cycle ultimately being broken and most importantly, two lost souls finding their deserved happy ending within each other.

The End

Made in the USA
Middletown, DE
26 July 2019